Trouble
According to
Humphrey

For more **Humphrey** adventures, look for

The World
According to Humphrey

Friendship
According to Humphrey

Trouble
According to
Humphrey

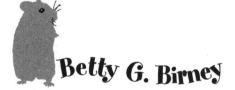

Betty G. Birney

G. P. Putnam's Sons

G. P. PUTNAM'S SONS
A division of Penguin Young Readers Group.
Published by The Penguin Group.
Penguin Group (USA) Inc., 375 Hudson Street, New York, NY 10014, U.S.A.
Penguin Group (Canada), 90 Eglinton Avenue East, Suite 700, Toronto, Ontario,
Canada M4P 2Y3 (a division of Pearson Penguin Canada Inc.).
Penguin Books Ltd, 80 Strand, London WC2R 0RL, England.
Penguin Ireland, 25 St. Stephen's Green, Dublin 2, Ireland
(a division of Penguin Books Ltd.).
Penguin Group (Australia), 250 Camberwell Road, Camberwell, Victoria 3124, Australia
(a division of Pearson Australia Group Pty Ltd).
Penguin Books India Pvt Ltd, 11 Community Centre, Panchsheel Park,
New Delhi—110 017, India.
Penguin Group (NZ), Cnr Airborne and Rosedale Roads, Albany, Auckland
1310, New Zealand (a division of Pearson New Zealand Ltd).
Penguin Books (South Africa) (Pty) Ltd, 24 Sturdee Avenue, Rosebank,
Johannesburg 2196, South Africa.
Penguin Books Ltd, Registered Offices: 80 Strand, London WC2R 0RL, England.

Published simultaneously in Canada. Printed in the United States of America.
Designed by Gina DiMassi and Katrina Damkoehler. Text set in Stempel Schneidler.

Library of Congress Cataloging-in-Publication Data
Birney, Betty G. Trouble according to Humphrey / Betty G. Birney.   p. cm.
Summary: Humphrey, the pet hamster of Longfellow School's Room 26,
relates the ups and downs experienced by his human classmates as they begin
a project to create a model town complete with houses and community services.
[1. Hamsters-Fiction. 2. Schools-Fiction. 3. Interpersonal relations-Fiction.] I. Title.
PZ7.B52285Tr 2007   [Fic]-dc22   2006003604
ISBN 978-0-399-24505-3
1 3 5 7 9 10 8 6 4 2
First Impression

To my son,
Walshe Hinson Birney,
who is as big-hearted
and clever as Humphrey—
but a lot taller!

❧

Special thanks to
Dr. Christina Swindall,
Judy Brady and the
Studio City Animal Hospital,
Studio City, California;
and to Stephanie Kelly
of Slidell, Louisiana.

Contents

Before the Trouble

W elcome to our brand-new town!"
Mrs. Brisbane's voice woke me from my cozy
afternoon doze. Was I dreaming when I heard her mention a new town? Had we moved while I was having my
afternoon nap?

Staying awake is a constant problem for a classroom
hamster like me. After all, hamsters are nocturnal, which
means we're sleepier in the daytime than at night. I always try hard to keep up with my fellow students in
Room 26. However, I'd spent the long Presidents' Day
Weekend at Kirk Chen's house. His whole family is
funny like he is. It was hard to get much sleeping done
there since I was laughing all the time.

But with Mrs. Brisbane's announcement, I was suddenly wide-awake. I looked around and saw that I was
in the same old Room 26 in my same old cage on the
table next to the window. Og the Frog's same old glass
house sat next to mine.

Around me were the usual tables and the familiar

students like Speak-Up-Sayeh, Lower-Your-Voice-A.J. and Wait-for-the-Bell-Garth. Mrs. Brisbane stood in front of the class as usual.

I guess I wasn't the only one who was confused. "What new town?" Heidi Hopper asked.

"Please Raise-Your-Hand-Heidi," Mrs. Brisbane said. "Since we are studying how communities work, I thought it was time to create our own community of Room Twenty-sixville."

Whew! I was relieved because I love our classroom right where it is and I wasn't in the mood to move.

"BOING!" said Og in his twangy voice. I guess he was relieved, too.

"We've been studying about what makes a community—right?" asked Mrs. Brisbane.

YES-YES-YES, I'd learned a lot about communities recently. First, I learned that there are two *m*'s in the word. I'm trying to remember that in case it shows up on a spelling test in the future. I'd learned that a community isn't just a place on a map, it's also made up of the people who live there. (I'm sure Mrs. Brisbane meant to include animals, too, but forgot to mention us.)

I'd also learned that everyone's job helps the community in some way or another. Police officers and fire fighters work to protect us. Some people sell books or clothes or even wonderful pets like me! Some people grow and sell food, some keep the streets clean and others, like Aldo, our custodian, keep the classrooms clean. Doctors take care of people when they are sick and dentists help folks keep their teeth healthy.

Then there's the biggest job of all: teacher. Teachers like Mrs. Brisbane help us learn about things we wouldn't know otherwise, such as the life cycle of a frog (though I still can't picture Og as a tadpole), how to write a poem and the way to add and subtract big numbers. Sometimes my paw gets tired from writing down really long problems in the tiny notebook I keep hidden behind my mirror, but I keep writing anyway because it's important.

My mind wandered while Mrs. Brisbane continued to talk about all we'd learned until I realized—oh, no!—I wasn't listening at all! If I kept daydreaming, I'd end up like Pay-Attention-Art Patel, who only paid attention in class about half the time and whose recent grades, I'm sorry to say, were dreadful. Not at all like Speak-Up-Sayeh, the quiet girl who always paid attention and got the best grades in class. (Better than mine, I have to admit.)

There I was again, my mind wandering to Art's problems instead of listening to Mrs. Brisbane. I hopped up on my ladder and vowed to listen to every word she said.

"It's one thing to talk about a community and another thing to be part of one," the teacher was saying. "So that's why I decided to create our own community here. We'll lay out our town right in this classroom and everyone will have a job."

Garth's hand shot up. "Will we get paid?"

"Not in money. You will get points for doing your jobs correctly and extra points for doing your job especially well."

Another hand went up. Mrs. Brisbane called on Don't-Complain-Mandy Payne. "I don't like the name Room Twenty-sixville," she said.

I don't think Mandy realizes how much she complains.

Mrs. Brisbane smiled. "Do you have a better name?"

Mandy scratched the tip of her nose. "Brisbaneville?"

"I don't want to name it after me," said the teacher. "Besides, there already is a famous town named Brisbane. It's in Australia and they pronounce it 'Brisbin'"

"Maybe we should call it Boringville," a low voice muttered.

"I-Heard-That-Kirk," Mrs. Brisbane said. "It was a rude thing to say. Do you really think school is boring?"

"Sorry. I was making a joke." I believed him because Kirk is such a big joker. He's also a quick thinker. "Og looks pretty bored," he said.

All heads—including mine—turned to gaze at Og, who sat completely motionless on his rock, staring into space without even blinking.

"Og is a frog," Mrs. Brisbane said. "He always looks that way."

I'm never completely sure what Og thinks, but *I* don't think Room 26 is a boring place at all. I decided to squeak up on the subject, so I leaped up and grabbed on to a leafy tree branch our teacher's husband, Mr. Brisbane, put in my cage. He was always adding new and interesting things to my home, like my ladders and a large cage extension.

4

Mrs. Brisbane turned toward me. "Humphrey certainly doesn't seem bored."

I loudly squeaked, "NO-NO-NO," and jumped to another branch.

"Let's call it Humphreyville!" That was definitely A.J.'s loud voice and this time he forgot to raise his hand, too.

"Humphreyville!" Voices burst out from around the room, along with chuckles and giggles.

"Humphreyville?" Mrs. Brisbane thought it over. Unfortunately, it was hard to think because Gail had gone into one of her giggling fits.

"Stop-Giggling-Gail," said the teacher. "Please. Now what do the rest of you think. Miranda?"

Miranda Golden—or Golden-Miranda, as I like to think of her—didn't hesitate a bit. "I love the name!"

"Sayeh? What do you think?"

For once, quiet Speak-Up-Sayeh didn't have any trouble speaking up. "Yes, it sounds like a real place."

"What is it again?" Pay-Attention-Art asked.

"Humphreyville," Sayeh told him.

"I never heard of a town named after a hamster," said Art.

Well, I may be a hamster, but I'm no ordinary hamster. I am an exceptionally cute Golden Hamster (I've been told) who happens to know how to read and write. Not that anyone knows about that except me. Or the fact that my cage has a lock-that-doesn't-lock so I can come and go as I please when no one's looking.

"Humphreyville," Art repeated. "Sounds pretty good."

I saw lots of heads nodding and heard murmuring around the class that sounded as if people were agreeing.

Imagine—a whole town named after me! I leaped onto my wheel and began spinning with joy.

"Why don't we take a vote?" asked Mrs. Brisbane. "All those in favor of naming our community 'Humphreyville,' raise your hands."

While I was spinning, I could see hands going up. Even Heidi remembered to raise her hand. Every hand was raised except one: Tabitha's. I stopped spinning.

Tabitha was the new girl in our class and I thought she liked me. I'd even helped her make friends with Seth, although she didn't actually know it. I have some sneaky, squeaky ways of making things like that happen.

"Tabitha, do you have another suggestion for a name?" Mrs. Brisbane asked.

"No," said Tabitha. "I like Humphreyville. I'm just afraid Og will be jealous."

Jealous! I hadn't thought about that, even though when Mrs. Brisbane brought Og in as a second classroom pet, I'd been jealous of him. It's embarrassing to admit it, but it's true.

"That's something to think about, isn't it? After all, if we named our community 'Tabithaville,' the other students might be jealous," the teacher agreed.

"Yeah, and it's hard to say," Heidi blurted out.

"Heidi, you simply must remember to raise your

hand!" Mrs. Brisbane had helped a lot students change their bad habits. Somehow, she'd never been able to get Heidi to remember to raise her hand.

"Now, class, why don't we let Og decide?" The teacher walked over to the frog's glass house. "Og, do you vote for Humphreyville?"

I wasn't expecting much, because I'd learned that Og, being a frog, has an unusual way of expressing himself. His "BOINGs" are nothing like the energetic squeaks of a hamster or the giggles and shouts of the kids. In fact, sometimes Og doesn't communicate at all. Still, he and I had learned to be friends. So I wouldn't have been surprised if he just continued to sit motionless, as usual.

But that's not what he did at all! Instead, he started leaping up and down on his rock, splashing water up on Mrs. Brisbane's chin. "BOING-BOING-BOING!" he twanged as only Og can do.

The students laughed uproariously. Even Mrs. Brisbane chuckled as she wiped the water off. "Thank you for your vote, Og. Now let's try again. All in favor of naming our new community 'Humphreyville,' raise your hands."

This time every hand went up, including Tabitha's. Whew! She liked me after all. Og stopped leaping and splashing and sat quietly on his rock again.

Mrs. Brisbane looked pleased. "Welcome, class, to the town of Humphreyville!" She wrote the name on the board in great big letters. "And to keep track of the progress of our town, we'll be starting a daily newspaper. I think *The Humphreyville Herald* would be a good name, don't you?"

My friends all agreed!

My heart hopped around in my chest like a happy frog. Had any hamster ever been honored like this before? Probably not. I decided right then and there that I would try to remain as humble as possible and do whatever I could to make Humphreyville the BEST-BEST-BEST town in the world!

I jumped on my wheel and spun for a while until I realized that Mrs. Brisbane was still talking. "There's a whole lot more to building a community than finding a name."

I stopped spinning and started listening.

"What's the first thing you need when you move to a new place?"

I knew what I'd need: a cage. There was no point in raising my paw since I never get called on, but a lot of other hands went up. Mrs. Brisbane called on Repeat-It-Please-Richie.

"A car," he said. "Or a truck to carry all the stuff you're moving."

"What if you didn't own anything at all?" asked the teacher. "What would you need first?"

"Bargainmart!" Richie said. Everybody laughed. I figured Bargainmart must be some kind of store, like Pet-O-Rama.

"I think you're jumping ahead. Tabitha, did you have your hand up?"

Tabitha nodded. "You'd need a place to live. A house."

"Or a tent!" Heidi blurted out.

"Very good," said Mrs. Brisbane, ignoring Heidi's outburst. "Something like a house. Your first assignment is to design a place that represents where you would live in the town. You can draw a picture or make a model out of clay or build it out of cardboard. Be creative and think about what kind of home you'd like for yourself in Humphreyville."

The bell rang. "We'll have math after recess and then we'll get to work on your homes."

Recess is a time when my fellow classmates all go out and play. It must be fun because my friends usually come back laughing and joking. At this time of year—late February—they also come back with rosy cheeks and red noses.

I always stay inside and try to get some exercise, climbing my ladder or spinning on my wheel. I must admit, sometimes I go in my sleeping hut for a nice nap because remember, I am nocturnal.

On this day, when Mrs. Brisbane wasn't paying attention, I sneaked my notebook into my sleeping hut and thought about what kind of house I'd build. I loved my cage, but sometimes I'd think about the fancy houses they sold at Pet-O-Rama. One was a Chinese pagoda and one was like a TALL-TALL-TALL castle. Ms. Mac, the substitute teacher and superb human being who first brought me from the pet store to Room 26 of Longfellow School, couldn't afford one of those, which was okay with me. Anything Ms. Mac did was fine with me. Yet, it was fun to think about my perfect house.

After all, if you have a whole town named after you, you should have a nice place to live!

NEW TOWN IN ROOM 26 TO BE NAMED AFTER CLASSROOM HAMSTER!

Houses will be going up in Humphreyville within a week, teacher predicts.

𝕿he 𝕳umphreyville 𝕳erald

The Problem with Paul

Humphreyville wasn't the only thing new in Room 26 that Tuesday. Once everyone was seated after recess, Mrs. Brisbane opened the door and in walked a small boy I'd never seen before. He stood very straight and held his chin high. "Welcome, Paul," the teacher said.

All of my classmates turned to stare at the boy, who stared right back at them. I craned my neck to get a look at him. All I could tell was that this Paul looked VERY-VERY-VERY serious.

"Class, some of you might know Paul Fletcher from Miss Loomis's class. He's going to be coming into our class for math every day from now on."

"He's a year behind us!" That was Heidi Hopper, of course.

Gail started to giggle but stopped herself, although I'm pretty sure Paul noticed. His chin sagged for a second.

"Heidi, please. Paul is an excellent math student and Mr. Morales asked if he could sit in on our class. I expect

11

you to treat him like any other classmate and be as help-ful as possible. Some of you probably already know Paul, don't you?"

Mrs. Brisbane waited. Very slowly, Art raised his hand.

"He lives across the street from me." Art kept doo-dling on a piece of paper. He was a great doodler. If I doodled as much as he did, I'd fill up my whole notebook in a day. Unlike Seth, who had a hard time sitting still, Art sat quietly but his pencil was always moving.

"Let's pull up a chair next to you. Here, Paul." Paul sat, though he and Art didn't look at each other. "Why don't we go around the room and introduce ourselves?"

One by one, my classmates said their names. Gail giggled when she told her name. Richie mumbled and Mrs. Brisbane had to say, "Repeat-It-Please-Richie." A.J. said his name extra loud, and Sayeh said, "I am Sayeh Nasiri. Welcome, Paul." That was nice.

When they were finished, I squeaked out, "And I am Humphrey!"

Mrs. Brisbane laughed and said, "I guess Humphrey wants to make sure you meet him, too. And Og, our frog, of course."

Og silently stared out of his glass house. Sometimes I wish he acted a little friendlier.

Mrs. Brisbane quickly launched into math class with a difficult problem for us to work out. Everybody went to work except me. I was too busy watching Paul writing like crazy. Mrs. Brisbane walked around the room to see how each student was working out the problem.

"Good, Heidi. Make sure those numbers line up," she said. "That's perfect, Sayeh." She told A.J. and Tabitha to try again.

When she saw Paul's answer, she smiled and said, "Excellent, Paul."

When she saw Art's answer, she stopping smiling and said, "Needs work, Art. Try going back to that first step and starting over."

I watched the two boys as the teacher did more explaining.

Art hadn't done well with his problem and he looked unhappy.

Paul had done REALLY-REALLY-REALLY well with his problem, but he looked unhappy, too!

At the end of all her explaining, Mrs. Brisbane told us that we'd have a test the next week and handed out a study sheet.

"Eeek!" I squeaked. I didn't mean to—I just realized that I'd been paying so much attention to Art and Paul that I hadn't listened to the teacher at all.

You should always listen to your teacher.

"Any questions?" she asked.

Paul raised his hand and she called on him. "What is Humphreyville?" he asked.

"It's our town we're creating for social studies."

"Oh," said Paul.

"Well, if there are no other questions, you may go,

Paul. We'll see you tomorrow!" Mrs. Brisbane used her especially cheery voice.

Paul didn't waste any time grabbing his notebook and hurrying out of Room 26.

I liked Paul, but I wasn't sure that he liked Room 26 very much.

〜•〜

By the next day, Humphreyville was taking shape. My fellow students had already begun to build their homes. Oh, there were so many different kinds! A.J. made a house out of blocks. He didn't care if somebody knocked it over because he could build it up again. Garth made a log cabin. Seth's "house" was a spaceship—cool! Golden-Miranda drew a picture of a purple castle (she deserves a castle). Heidi, true to her word, made a blue tent with pink and yellow polka dots.

Sayeh built a tall apartment building. She said since Humphreyville would be such a popular place, we would need a lot of places for people to live. Mandy's house was very tall and narrow. She explained that each floor was for a different member of her family. Unfortunately, it kept tipping over.

By far, the house that got the most attention was Art's. He used small plastic bricks, metal springs, sprockets and things-I-don't-know-the-names-of to build a house that had a big slide coming out of the attic, inner rooms that revolved like a merry-go-round and train tracks that went right through the middle.

"I believe Art's house will put Humphreyville on the

map," Mrs. Brisbane said. I think he got the first "A" on that project that he's had all year. I sure gave him an "A."

When Paul came into class for math, he sat next to Art, although they ignored each other completely. It sounds strange, but Paul looked even smaller when he walked out of Room 26 than when he walked in.

⌣⌣⌣

On Wednesday evening, I scribbled in my notebook, working on the drawing of my house. It got dark early. Luckily, I could sketch by the light of the streetlamp outside the window. Of course, the sound of the crickets (Og's special treats) going "CHIRRUP-CHIRRUP" sometimes made it hard to concentrate.

Suddenly, I was blinded by bright lights. "Surprise, surprise! Aldo has arrived!" My eyes adjusted to the light and there was our friendly custodian, Aldo Amato, bowing from the waist. I quickly slipped my notebook behind my mirror.

"Greetings, Aldo," I shouted. I knew it came out "SQUEAK-SQUEAK-SQUEAK," but Aldo always seemed to understand me.

"Hello, Humphrey! Howdy-do, Og!" Aldo pulled his cleaning cart into the room, took out his broom and started sweeping. He stopped as soon as he started. "*Mamma mia,* what's all this?" he asked, looking around at the room.

"HUMPHREYVILLE," I squeaked loudly.

"BOING!" shouted Og.

I could see how surprised Aldo was and with good

reason. Since the night before, the whole room had changed. Tables with all the students' homes lined the back of the room and the rows between their seats had big signs on them with street names. My classmates had argued over—I mean *discussed*—what each street should be named. When Mrs. Brisbane suggested First Street, Second Street, and so forth, the students didn't like that idea. Then she'd suggested naming the streets after presidents, but my friends weren't interested in that, either.

"We want something that stands for us," Garth said. "Names that are things we like."

Now the growing town of Humphreyville had Soccer Street and Basketball Avenue, Video Game Way and Recess Lane, as well as Pizza Place and Taco Boulevard.

Aldo's big black mustache bounced heartily as he laughed and looked around. WELCOME TO HUMPHREYVILLE, a sign announced in big bright letters. The table where Og and I live had some grassy material on it with a sign that read, OG THE FROG NATURE PRESERVE.

I was glad they named something after Og, so he wouldn't feel jealous. Jealousy feels BAD-BAD-BAD.

Aldo started sweeping again. "I'm lucky I get to clean Mrs. Brisbane's room every night, because I learn so much about being a teacher!" He had just returned to college so he could teach school, which was an excellent idea.

"Humphreyville!" he repeated again with a chuckle. "Looks like the perfect place to live!"

Aldo went about his work in his usual quick and efficient way, then pulled a chair up near my cage and took out his lunch bag. He always took his dinner break with Og and me and talked about his life. He talked about his wife, Maria, who worked at the bakery and had a beautiful smile. Lately, he talked a lot about college.

"Whew, Humphrey, I knew that school wouldn't be easy, but it's getting harder all the time," he said. "I'm lucky Maria is an understanding woman, because I hardly have any free time. I haven't even been bowling in weeks."

Although I wasn't completely sure I knew what "bowling" was, I knew it was something Aldo enjoyed. He chewed his sandwich thoughtfully for a moment. "Still, it will be worth it. I can be a teacher and work with kids and maybe have a house like one of these," he said, waving toward the back tables. "Like the one with the train tracks going through it."

He reached in his sandwich and pulled out a piece of lettuce. "Here's to your health, Humphrey." He pushed the lettuce into my cage.

I squeaked a heartfelt thanks.

"Sorry I don't have something for you, Og my man," he told my neighbor. "You're a lot pickier than Humphrey."

Picky? The frog eats *crickets! Yech.* Not nearly as appealing as the mealworms I enjoy.

Aldo hurried out the door with his squeaky cart. Although I was sorry my friend didn't have time to go bowling, I was glad he was going to be a teacher, like

Mrs. Brisbane. I could hardly believe that when I first met Mrs. Brisbane, I didn't think she was a very nice person. In fact, I thought she was out to get me. Now, she's one of my favorite humans—and I have a lot of favorite humans!

⚬～⚬

During the next few days, my classmates worked hard building up Humphreyville. Every day, Paul came in for math class. Though he sat next to Art, his neighbor never even looked at him. Every day, Paul left the classroom in a big hurry.

On Friday afternoon, it was time for Mrs. Brisbane to announce which student would be bringing me home for the weekend. It was always an exciting moment for my classmates and even more exciting for me. My whiskers wiggled wildly as I waited to find out where I'd be staying.

"Pick me," said Mandy, frantically waving her arm. "You've never let me take Humphrey home."

She was right. I'd been home with many of my friends—some of them even twice—but I'd never gone home with Mandy.

"You haven't brought back the permission slip I sent home with you," said Mrs. Brisbane.

Mandy let out a huge sigh, then said, "My folks have been busy."

"Well, tell them I'm waiting for their signatures. Now, I believe Seth is scheduled to take Humphrey home this weekend."

18

Sit-Still-Seth Stevenson was so excited, he jiggled his chair until it actually tipped over. Luckily, he wasn't hurt.

"Try to stay calm," said Mrs. Brisbane.

"I WILL-WILL-WILL." I covered my mouth with my paws when I realized that she had been talking to Seth. I made a mistake. After all, I'm only human. I mean . . . only a hamster. (Which is a very good thing.)

NO HOUSING SHORTAGE
IN HUMPHREYVILLE!

Building boom keeps Room 26 students hopping.
Population swells as Paul Fletcher joins math class.

𝕿he 𝕳umphreyville 𝕳erald

The Situation with the Stevensons

The reason I used to think Seth's full name was Sit-Still-Seth was because he always wiggles in his chair and Mrs. Brisbane always reminds him to sit still. He really does try, but he has so much energy, he just has to move. I guess that's why he loves sports a lot, both playing them and watching them, along with our other sports fan in Room 26, Tabitha.

As much as I like Seth, I was hoping his whole family didn't fidget and squirm as much as he did. I always have my wheel to work off my excess energy. Too bad Seth doesn't have one, too.

On Friday, Seth's mom, June, drove us home without as much as a twitch. She did tell her son to quit bouncing up and down on the seat, which I appreciated, as car rides always make me queasy even without Seth's jiggling and joggling.

"Thanks for picking me up, Mom," Seth said. "I thought Grandma would do it."

"I was afraid she'd have trouble with the cage. The

shop wasn't busy and Carolyn covered for me. I'll do the same for her next week." She laughed. "I'll be glad when your sister can drive you."

Seth bounced a little higher. "I won't!" he exclaimed.

Once we were home and I was placed in the den on a big table, I saw the other members of Seth's family. His sister was a teenager named Lucinda and Grandma was an older lady who I later figured out was June's mom.

"Want to meet Humphrey?" Seth asked his sister.

She turned up her nose. "Hamsters are for children," she said, and walked away. "I'm going to write in my journal now, so please don't disturb me."

"Don't worry, I won't!" I squeaked at her. Hamsters are for children! Try telling that to Principal Morales or Aldo or even Mrs. Brisbane.

The older woman slowly approached the cage and leaned over to get a closer look at me—but not too close.

"Don't worry, Grandma. He won't hurt you," said Seth.

"Is it clean?" she asked.

"Probably cleaner than I am," Seth joked.

Grandma didn't crack a smile. "I'm afraid that might be all too true," she said. She backed away from my cage and left the room.

"You'd better give him some fresh water," Seth's mom suggested. "And some food."

At least Seth's mom didn't call me an "it," which I always appreciate.

Once I was settled in, Seth started playing video

games. He didn't merely sit and play. He bounced and bobbed, he shook and shimmied, he rattled and rocked. I was feeling kind of woozy, so I crawled into my sleeping hut for a nice doze. I woke up when Seth's mom announced that dinner was ready. Luckily, the den had a big wide opening right into the kitchen, which is where the family sat down to eat.

Dinners at my classmates' houses are always fun, too—there are yummy smells and interesting things to hear, all about one person's day at work and another person's day at school. Some people were loud while they ate, like Lower-Your-Voice-A.J. and his family. Some people were quiet, like Tabitha and her foster mom.

Seth's family didn't talk much, but when they did, it was always about one subject: Seth.

"Can't you sit still?" asked Lucinda, in a superior tone of voice I didn't care for.

"I am sitting still," said Seth.

"You are not! You bumped the table. See, my water spilled," his sister replied.

"Do try and be calm, honey," Seth's mom said.

"In my day," Grandma began, then started over in a much more dramatic voice. "In *my* day, boys and girls had to sit still at the table without saying a word. That was what we called manners. Are you listening?"

"Yes, ma'am," said Seth, sounding quite miserable.

Everything was quiet for a while except for the clinking and clanking of knives and forks (I don't know why humans need those when they have a perfectly good set of paws, like I do). Then Lucinda exclaimed, "He's doing it again!"

"What?" said Seth.

"You know what. Shaking your legs."

"Sorry, *Cindy*," he said.

"My name is Lucinda!" she answered icily.

"You used to like to be called Cindy."

"Well, I don't now."

Seth and his family were silent for a while until Lucinda clanked her fork loudly and said, "Oh, really! If you bump that table leg one more time, I'll—"

"It was an accident," said Seth.

"Kids, please." Seth's mom sounded tired.

"In my day," Grandma began again. "In *my* day, children were not allowed to argue at the table."

"I'll bet Seth can't stay still for one minute," said Lucinda in a nasty voice.

"I'll bet you can't stay still for two minutes," said Seth.

"June, you should not allow your children to gamble," Grandma grumbled. "In *my* day—"

"Mother, you're not helping," said June, which was true.

"—my mother wouldn't allow us to make bets."

This conversation was getting on my nerves, so I hopped on my wheel to try and relax. Unfortunately, my wheel always makes an annoying SCREECH!

"What on earth is that creature doing?" asked Grandma.

"He's on his exercise wheel. It's good for him," Seth replied.

Grandma sniffed loudly. "I guess nobody around here can sit still except me."

"Well, *I* certainly can," Lucinda objected.

"You move as much as anybody," said Seth. "Look, you just blinked!"

"Blinking doesn't count! Banging the table like you do—that counts." Somebody, maybe Lucinda, banged a hand on the table. I could tell because the dishes rattled.

Someone else—I'm guessing it was Seth—banged a hand on the table, too.

"That's enough!" Seth's mom sounded as if she was about to explode. "Night after night, all you do is bicker about who's sitting still and who's not and who's right and who's wrong! Well, I've had it. We're going to leave the table and go into the den and settle this once and for all."

"For goodness' sakes! And let my dinner get cold?" Grandma asked in a sad little voice.

"It's a salad. It's supposed to be cold," said June. I'd heard irritated moms before, but she sounded as if she'd really had it.

She marched into the den, and surprisingly, Lucinda, Seth and Grandma followed.

"Now, just sit down on the couch," she said firmly.

"In my day, children—even adult children—didn't address their parents in that tone of voice," said Grandma.

"You don't have to be in this contest, Mother. You

24

can go finish your salad. This is between Seth and Lucinda."

Grandma slowly moved back toward the kitchen, then hesitated. "What contest?"

"The Sitting-Still Contest to see who can sit the longest without moving."

"What does the winner get?" asked Lucinda.

June thought for a few seconds. "A pair of tickets for the winner and a friend to the movies tomorrow. I'll also provide popcorn money and transportation."

"I could take my friend Adele," said Grandma. "I'm in." She planted herself on the couch right between Lucinda and Seth.

"Can we take anyone we want?" asked Lucinda.

"You may take anyone who is old enough to go to the movies and behave." Boy, Seth's mom really meant business.

I'd been so caught up in this whole fascinating discussion, I didn't realize I was spinning on my wheel. June twirled around and pointed an accusing finger at me.

"You have to sit still, too, Humphrey."

I stopped cold and tumbled off my wheel. There's a trick to getting off a spinning object, which I temporarily forgot.

"Is Humphrey in the contest?" asked Seth.

"I guess he can't go to the movies. But if Humphrey stays still longer than anyone, he gets a nice big chunk of whatever he likes."

"Apples!" I squeaked.

Seth looked thoughtful. "He likes fruit," he said. Smart guy!

June sounded a bit calmer. "Let's all relax for a minute and take a few deep breaths."

"Mom, can we move Humphrey's cage closer? I'm going to concentrate on him. As long as I stare at him, I think I can do it," said Seth.

"Any objections?" asked June.

"I don't care, as long as I don't have to touch it," said Lucinda. "Besides, hamsters never stop moving. Look at it."

I realized that she was right. We hamsters do tend to be as jumpy as Seth. Even if we're standing still, our whiskers are wiggling or our noses are twitching. However, if my keeping still could help Seth . . . well, he was a classmate, and in Room 26 we stick together.

Seth's mom pushed my table closer to the couch and checked her watch. "I have a second hand on my watch. In thirty seconds I'll say 'freeze.' At that point you must stop all movement. You'll be eliminated as soon as you move."

"Who gets to be the judge?" asked Grandma.

"I do," said June in a voice that no one would want to argue with. No one did, least of all—me!

"Can we blink?" asked Lucinda.

"Yes, you can blink and you can breathe. That's it."

June's watch was very quiet but I could almost feel it TICK-TICK-TICK-ing away the seconds, the way the clock in Room 26 does when everyone goes home and it's awfully quiet.

26

I was pretty worried because I was looking straight ahead at Seth and he was tapping his fingers on the table. Lucinda seemed quite determined with her arms folded tightly against her body. Grandma sat up very straight. (I bet people in "her day" always did.)

"Ten, nine, eight, seven, six, five, four, three, two—freeze!" said June.

I froze. The Sitting-Still Contest had begun!

Oh, dear, oh, dear. If you don't have whiskers, you have no idea how difficult it is to keep them from moving. I stared straight ahead at Seth, who was as motionless as Og is when he sits on his rock. In fact, I tried to pretend I *was* a frog, which is not an easy thing for a hamster to do.

"You can do it . . . you can do it. . . ." I sent out my thoughts to Seth. Even though he probably couldn't hear my thoughts, I figured as long as I could stay still, maybe he could, too. My tail felt like twitching and my nose was itching and I'd never gone so long without moving. Seth stared at me and I stared back.

After a while, Grandma's chin dropped and her head bobbed up and down. Grandma had moved and she didn't even know it because she was asleep! She began to snore softly.

"One down," said June, keeping her gaze fixed firmly on Lucinda, Seth and me.

No one else had made a move yet and neither did I, although seeing Grandma asleep like that made me not only want to wiggle, it made me want to giggle.

Seth was as frozen as a statue and I was proud of

him. However, Lucinda looked like she was made of solid steel.

TICK-TICK-TICK. That imaginary clock sounded loud in my brain. Amazingly, Seth still hadn't moved a muscle. I tried to keep my gaze firmly on him, though once in a while I glanced at Lucinda. I was beginning to believe the girl had turned to stone. Suddenly, I saw her blink. Okay, blinking was okay, but this was like a double blink. Like a wink. Followed by another and another. Pretty soon she was blinking both eyes, hard.

Aha, I thought. She's trying to throw me off. Because she thinks that if she throws me off, I'll throw Seth off. Which would be a shame because even if Seth lost, he had already sat still longer than ever before.

Then it happened. Lucinda's head twitched and the blinking got even faster until she jumped up off the couch, holding her eye with one hand. "My contact! I've got something in my eye!" she wailed, and raced out of the room.

"Two down," said June, sounding less edgy than before. "I guess you're the winner, Seth."

Even then, Seth didn't blink an eye. He stared straight at me. At *me!* Now I got it—Seth was determined to stay still longer than I did.

I wanted to squeak with joy because Seth had done so well. But there was the matter of this little itch right next to my nose. It was a little itch that grew into a bigger, more irritating itch that grew into an UNBEARABLE TICKLING ITCH. At last, I reached up to scratch it.

"Three down," said June. "Seth, you *are* the winner!"

Seth leaped up from the couch and jumped up and down, making V's with his fingers. "I won! Tell Lucinda! I won!"

Grandma's head jerked up as she awoke with a start. "Whazzit?" she asked groggily. "Did I win?"

"No, Mother. You moved first when you fell asleep."

"Perfectly ridiculous. I was just resting my eyes."

"Seth won!" June gave her son a hug. "Now we know you can control yourself if you put your mind to it."

"I guess," said Seth. He looked worried. I bet he was wondering if was going to have to sit like a statue forever.

"Not all the time, of course," said June. I do believe parents can sometimes read their children's minds. "Just when you need to, like during a test."

Seth sighed. "I'll try harder, I promise. Mom, can I call Tabitha and ask if she can come see that football movie tomorrow?" asked Seth.

"I'll call her mother after dinner," said June.

Lucinda wandered in, rubbing her eye. "Stupid contact lens. I don't suppose we can have a rematch."

"Anytime you want," said Seth confidently.

"*I'll* have a rematch," said Grandma.

"No rematches," June stated firmly. "Now, what do you say we order some pizza to go with that salad?"

"They didn't have pizza in your day, Grandma, did they?" Lucinda asked.

"Pizza! In my day, we *invented* pizza! Pepperoni and onions for me, hold the peppers."

I was glad they weren't arguing anymore, but I hoped

29

I wouldn't have to hold the peppers. (They're way too spicy for me.)

⚬⌣•⌣⚬

The next day, as promised, June took Seth and Tabitha to see the football movie at the mall (a place I've never been) and took Lucinda shopping. Grandma stayed home. That made me a teensy bit nervous, because I had a feeling that in her day, people didn't have hamsters. Or if they did, they did something worse with them than put them in a cage!

For a while, she ignored me and watched a couple of programs on television where grown-ups sat around and argued with each other. Whew! I'm glad Mrs. Brisbane doesn't let the kids in Room 26 argue all the time. I guess even Grandma got tired of those shows, because she turned the TV off and came over to my cage.

"Let's get a good look at you, young man." She pulled her glasses out of her pocket and leaned in to examine me. "Well, you're just a little bit of a fellow, aren't you? Not good for much, I guess."

Me—Humphrey the Hamster—not good for much! I decided to show Grandma a thing or two. I scurried up my ladder, leaped onto a tree branch and hung there from one paw. It was a trick that had never failed to please humans. So far, Grandma wasn't anything like the other humans I'd met. I swung myself up to my bridge ladder, dashed across it and dove onto my wheel. WHOA-WHOA-WHOA—I almost lost my balance, but I managed to get the wheel going without falling over.

"Why, aren't you Mr. Show-off?" said Grandma. "Quite the daredevil."

Then she did something surprising. She chuckled.

Since I was on a roll, I hopped off my wheel, grabbed onto my ladder and hung on with both paws, swinging my body back and forth.

"Ha-ha! Reminds me of a song we sang as kids." Amazingly, Grandma began to sing.

He floats through the air with the greatest of ease,
The daring young man on the flying trapeze. . . .
His actions are da-da,
Da-da-da-da-dee,
And my heart he has stolen away!

It was an excellent song. She had a pretty good voice, too, even if she couldn't remember all the words. I liked being the daring young hamster on the flying trapeze.

"I'd almost forgotten that old song. I'll tell you, Humphrey—that's your name, isn't it?"

"Of course!" I squeaked.

"My name is Dot Larrabee. Humphrey, when I was young, we used to sing all the time. Now kids just listen to music. In my day, we made our own."

I dropped down from my "trapeze" and listened.

"And for fun we'd go to the roller rink." Dot's eyes lit up as she talked. "There used to be a roller skating rink where the mall is now. Next door was an amusement park with a Ferris wheel and a merry-go-round. You could go on a couple of rides, maybe have some cotton candy or a snow cone. Once I saw a dancing bear there. A man would play the accordion and the bear would really dance! Now all there is to do is spend money on clothes. Who cares about clothes?"

"I don't!" I was squeaking the truth. I was perfectly happy with my fur coat.

"I've seen a lot of changes in my day," said Dot. "But nobody wants to hear about my life."

"I do!" I squeaked, and I meant it.

She smiled again. "You're a chipper fellow. I like you, kiddo. I really do."

And I REALLY-REALLY-REALLY liked Dot.

"We lived in a yellow house with white trim, down on Alder Street. It was a small house with a nice big yard with trees to climb and places to play hide-and-seek. It was near the Dairy Maid, only back then, it was a little corner store."

Alder Street! Dairy Maid! That was right where I came from, next door to Pet-O-Rama!

"They tore all that down, that block of pretty houses. Put in a pet store and a music store or something. Right where I used to play when I was a girl."

They tore down her house to build Pet-O-Rama! I was learning a lot, because I'd imagined Pet-O-Rama had always been there at the corner of Fifth and Alder. My mind was a million miles away when I heard a door slam, followed by the stomping and clomping of feet.

"Mother?" June called out.

"I'm in here with Humphrey," said Dot.

June, Seth and Lucinda came into the den, all bundled up in coats, hats and scarves.

"You were probably smart to stay home," said June. "It's started to sleet!"

I wasn't exactly sure what sleet was, but it sounded COLD-COLD-COLD.

"Of course it has," said Dot. "Anybody with a lick of sense would expect it. Today's March first. And you know what they always say: March comes in like a lion and goes out like a lamb. Hardly ever fails. Why, in my day, we had three feet of snow on March first one year. I must have been ten. Or maybe eleven."

Seth and Lucinda rolled their eyes, as if to say, "There she goes again."

But when I looked at Dot, I saw a young girl gazing out of the window of a yellow house with white trim, watching the snowflakes fluttering down, thinking about a dancing bear.

ᴗ~ᴗ

Later that night, I was feeling especially nocturnal, so I decided to perform my daring-young-hamster-on-the-flying-trapeze routine for Seth. I leaped up, grabbed onto my bridge ladder and swung across it.

"If you were a human, you could be on the Olympic gymnastics team," said Seth, and it sounded like a very good thing.

"I wish Dad could see you," he continued. "He lives

in Arizona where it's warm all the time. He coaches high school basketball. I spend the whole summer there and boy, it's hot. I guess Mrs. Brisbane wouldn't let you stay for the whole summer." He seemed disappointed and I guess I was, too. I knew that the capital of Arizona is Phoenix—whew, that's not easy to spell—but I wanted to know what it would be like to live in a place where it was warm all the time.

I glanced out the window and, not only was it *not* warm, tiny pieces of ice were falling outside. Sleet!

<hr />

On Sunday, I saw an amazing sight: The trees outside the window were covered in ice, which glittered like diamonds when the sun came out in the afternoon. Dot stood at the window, admiring the display. "Yessir, March came in like a lion, so you know she'll go out like a lamb. Days like this when I was a kid, we'd go ice skating over on Dobbs' Pond. Don't kids do that anymore, June?"

June joined her mother at the window. "They paved that over and built houses there years ago, Mother."

"Fools! What do you bet they get water in the basements when it rains? You can't stop nature."

June called to Seth. "Did you see these trees? They're really beautiful."

Seth was watching a basketball game on TV. "I saw them," he said, but I knew he hadn't taken his eyes off the screen for the whole game.

June went into the kitchen, but Grandma stayed at the window, watching the sun shine though the icy branches.

"Skating on Dobbs Pond . . ." Dot sounded wistful.

If I had a choice, I'd be out there skating with her.

FREEZING RAIN AND SNOW
KEEP STUDENTS INSIDE
OVER THE WEEKEND!

Humphrey stays warm at Seth Stevenson's house.

𝕿he 𝕳umphreyville 𝕳erald

The Great Cage Catastrophe

The sun melted all the ice that Sunday afternoon. On Monday, it was cold and windy. "March comes in like a lion," Dot had said, and she sure was right. I shivered in my cage despite the heavy blanket that Seth put over it before he and his mom took me out to the car. Being chilly is one thing, but a lion can be big trouble. Was trouble blowing its way toward Room 26? (The answer is YES-YES-YES. I just didn't know it yet.)

It was warm and cozy back in the classroom. I tried to tell Og about my weekend at Seth's house, but Mrs. Brisbane had to "shush" me. During the spelling test, I was so busy watching Seth that I didn't concentrate as hard as I should have. Seth did a lot less fidgeting than usual, and I noticed when he started jiggling in his seat, he'd glance over at me for a second and settle down. Good job!

I graded my test and was shocked to see that I'd only gotten 79%. Sayeh, as usual, got 100%. I'm not sure what grade Seth got, but he was smiling. Whatever grade Art got, it must not have been good because a) he wasn't smiling and b) the teacher asked him to stay in during recess. *Everybody* knew what that meant.

Then, we had a surprise visit from Principal Morales. He's the Most Important Person at Longfellow School and a personal friend of mine ever since I spent a weekend at his house. Mr. Morales always wears a special tie. Today his tie had colorful little houses all over it.

"I hope you don't mind me dropping in on Humphreyville," he said. "I've heard so much about it, I had to see it for myself." He strolled past the tables, admiring the houses and the street signs, and ended up near my cage. "I can't think of a better name than the one you've picked."

"THANKS-THANKS-THANKS!" I squeaked. As usual it came out "SQUEAK-SQUEAK-SQUEAK," and everybody laughed.

"You're just in time for the next phase of our town-building," said Mrs. Brisbane. "Today, we're all going to get jobs."

I heard gasps and murmurs around the room and my mind was whirling. Mrs. Brisbane already had a job—being our teacher. I had a job—being the classroom pet to help students learn about other species. As Ms. Mac said when she first brought me to Room 26, "You can learn a lot about yourself by taking care of another species," and it was true. Now I shared the job with Og. But I sometimes wondered whether there was anything new for my friends to learn now that I'd been in class for a while.

My mind was spinning a bit too fast and I missed

some of what Mrs. Brisbane was saying. Something about people in a community contributing by doing specific jobs. She'd already started writing names of jobs on the chalkboard as students called them out:

Teacher
Police Officer
Fire Fighter

"That's what I want to do," Garth said, aiming an imaginary fire hose at A.J. and making loud squirting sounds.

"Garth . . . " Mrs. Brisbane used her warning voice and kept on writing.

Doctor
Nurse
Dentist

"Who needs a dentist?" joked Kirk, folding his lips over his teeth so he looked completely toothless. Gail giggled but Mrs. Brisbane ignored them both and kept going.

Shopkeeper
Farmer
Builder

"You left out one job," said Mr. Morales. "School principal. And I'd better get back to my job before Mrs. Brisbane gives me a new one!"

Everyone laughed as he left and the list-making continued.

When things quieted down, the teacher made her own suggestions. "I think we're forgetting a few other important jobs in a town. People to keep the electricity going and run grocery stores and gas stations."

"Car washes," said Seth.

"Car lots!" added A.J. "You can't wash your car until you buy one."

All these interesting jobs had my head whirling. I dashed into my sleeping hut and quickly wrote the list down in my secret notebook. I'm grateful that Ms. Mac gave me the little notebook and pencil when she first brought me to Room 26, before I met Mrs. Brisbane. After Ms. Mac moved to Brazil, she came back to visit and brought me a brand-new notebook. (Although I worry about what I'll do when I fill this one up, so I write extra-extra-small.)

Finally, Mrs. Brisbane said, "I think we have a good list here. Now, I'm going to assign jobs for Humphreyville."

The room was in an uproar as students called out the jobs they wanted.

"I'll be the Fire Chief!" said Garth.

Mandy frowned. "I don't want to clean the dirty old streets. Or wash dishes."

Mrs. Brisbane smiled. "These aren't exactly the kinds of jobs we're going to have in Humphreyville. You will have classroom jobs, based on the real jobs in a community." She walked over to the map, which was pulled down. "Here's the list I've made." She rolled the map UP-UP-UP and behind it on the chalkboard was a chart with a whole list of jobs I'd never even heard of before.

"Are you paying attention, Og?" I squeaked to my neighbor. "We're going to have new jobs!"

There was such a loud buzz in the room, Mrs. Brisbane had to say, "Shush," then "Class!" and "Quiet now!" before everyone calmed down.

"Listen carefully, please," she said. "The jobs will rotate on a weekly basis. So whatever your job is the first week, you'll have a different job next week. If you don't get the job you want the first time, you'll have another chance at it. You'll be graded on a point system. You'll get ten points for doing a good job. I will add extra points for doing an especially good job and subtract points if you don't do a good job. Understand?"

Heads nodded yes around the room and a few hands shot up. Mrs. Brisbane called on Mandy.

"If we like our jobs, why can't we keep them?" Mandy asked in her whiniest voice.

"Because I think you'll learn more by switching around."

Mrs. Brisbane turned and began filling in names next to the jobs listed.

Pencil Patrol—Heidi Hopper
Paper Monitor—A.J. Thomas
Door Monitor—Kirk Chen
Chalkboard Eraser—Gail Morgenstern
Energy Monitor—Art Patel

Line Monitor—Sayeh Nasiri
Plant Technician—Richie Rinaldi
Table Inspector—Mandy Payne
Animal Keeper—Miranda Golden
Teacher Assistant—Seth Stevenson
Homework Monitor—Tabitha Clark

Name after name, job after job, each one sounding more interesting than the next! Imagine erasing the chalkboard at the end of every day. Or being Mrs. Brisbane's actual assistant!

I was especially thrilled that Golden-Miranda was going to be in charge of Og and me because she takes such good care of us.

But not everyone was happy. Hands were raised. Kirk thought being the Door Monitor sounded boring. Heidi wanted to know what a Pencil Patrol Person did. When she heard she had to make sure the students had sharp pencils when they needed them, she didn't complain.

Mandy, on the other hand, did complain when she found out the Table Monitor was supposed to make sure everybody's work space was neat. "I don't want to clean up somebody else's mess." Mrs. Brisbane explained that she didn't have to clean up the mess. She just had to give a student a written notice stating that their work space needs straightening. If someone's table didn't get straightened, she was to report that student to Mrs. Brisbane.

"It's an important job," the teacher explained. Mandy seemed satisfied.

"Any more questions?" Mrs. Brisbane asked.

Art slowly raised his hand. "What's that Energy Monitor job?"

"At recess, lunch and the end of school, you make sure the lights are turned off to save electricity. When everybody comes back, you turn the lights on."

"That sounds easier than being a Table Monitor," Mandy argued.

"Don't worry," the teacher replied. "You'll all switch jobs at the end of the week. Okay, we'll start this afternoon."

When it was time for recess, my friends put on their coats and rushed outside. Pay-Attention-Art stayed behind as Mrs. Brisbane had requested. Once my classmates had cleared out, she went over and sat down next to him. In her hand was Art's spelling test.

"Art, about this F . . ."

My heart pounded. Art got an F! F as in Failure! F as in Flunking! F as in Family-being-really-mad if you bring home one of those on your report card!

"Art, I know math can be a problem for you, but you've always done better with your spelling. What happened?"

Art stared down at the table and shrugged his shoulders. "I goofed up."

"Did you study?"

"I forgot."

F as in Forgot-to-study!

"You've been forgetting a lot lately. What's on your mind?"

Art shrugged his shoulders again. "I don't know. I just think about stuff I like."

Mrs. Brisbane examined the elaborate house that Art had built, the one with the train tracks going through it. "Stuff like building this house?"

"Yeah. I like building things."

"And you're good at it. Look, I know you can do better than this. If I let you retake the test tomorrow, will you study for it tonight? Otherwise, I'll have to let your parents know about this F."

Art perked right up. "I'll study tonight. I promise!"

Mrs. Brisbane pushed back her chair and stood up. "Don't disappoint me, Art. Tonight, what are you going to do?"

"Study!" He sounded convincing to me.

"Good," the teacher said with a smile. "Now, why don't you get your coat and go on out to recess?"

Art didn't waste any time grabbing his coat and dashing out of the room. After he left, Mrs. Brisbane stopped smiling. "I hope you do study, Art," she said softly.

After school, I stared at the job list I'd written down. Good thing I had, too, since Gail was such an excellent Chalkboard Eraser, Mrs. Brisbane had to stop her before she erased the list of jobs. On the other hand, Art had not exactly been a great Energy Monitor. He left the lights on at the end of the day. I wished he'd pay more attention.

Usually, I would have been glad the lights were on so I could study my notebook. But I had something else on my mind. I turned to my neighbor.

"Og? Can you hear me?"

I heard the faintest splashing of water. At least I knew he was listening.

"I've been thinking about this job thing," I squeaked.

The splashing got louder. My small hamster voice couldn't be heard over the noise, so I opened my cage's lock-that-doesn't-lock. It looks like it's locked when a human closes my door, but I can easily open it from the inside. No one knows about it except Og, thank goodness! I couldn't have helped my friends and had so many adventures without that good old lock.

I scampered over to Og's house. "Our friends have helping kinds of jobs, like taking care of us. Even if we can't erase the chalkboard or turn off the lights, there must be something useful we can do."

"BOING!" Og jumped up alarmingly high.

"Mrs. Brisbane didn't even think of us. So we're going to have to find jobs of our own. Real jobs, like turning off the lights."

"BOING-BOING!" Og jumped up even higher.

"Good! You want a job, too. Is that what you're saying?"

"BOING-BOING-BOING!" My froggy friend was quite frantic, which was certainly unusual for him.

I didn't realize that he was actually trying to warn me until Aldo hurried into the room, pulling his cart. "What are the lights doing on? A waste of energy," he grumbled.

My heart was thumping so loudly, Aldo could probably hear it. I couldn't let anyone discover the secret about my lock! I madly dashed back to my cage and almost made it, too, but it's hard to stay ahead of Aldo.

"Hey, buddy, hold on, there!"

His big hand reached down and picked me up. "What are you doing out of your cage? This classroom could be a dangerous place for a small fellow like you. Somebody could have squashed you or something."

He gently placed me back in my cage and closed the door, checking to see that the lock was firmly locked. "It seems okay," he said. "But just to be safe, I'll give you some extra protection." He searched around until he found a large paper clip, which he straightened out. Then he bent it around the door of my cage.

"EEK!" I squeaked. I was *really* locked in now.

Aldo stroked his mustache thoughtfully. "Somebody must have left your door open. I wonder who took care of you today?"

He thought for a minute, then took out a piece of paper and sat down to write a note to Mrs. Brisbane. "I'd better tell her that whoever's supposed to take care of you didn't do a very good job."

I swallowed hard. Golden-Miranda had the job of

Animal Keeper and no one took better care of pets than she did. (Even if she personally owned a scary dog named Clem.)

"NO-NO-NO!" I squeaked, trying to make Aldo understand that he was making a big mistake. "Not Miranda!"

For once, Aldo didn't get it. "I know, pal. It must have been pretty scary being out of the cage like that. Mrs. Brisbane will take care of it." He folded the note and put it on her desk.

My stomach was bumpy and jumpy, the way it feels when I have to ride the school bus with somebody. Aldo finished cleaning and ate his dinner, but I was so upset, I wasn't even interested in the carrot he offered me.

Aldo got up and pushed his cart toward the door. "Lights out, guys. Gotta save that energy."

After he left and the room was dark again, I squeaked to Og. "Thanks for trying to warn me, Oggy. Next time, I'll pay more attention."

"BOING-BOING," he replied.

"I've got to get over to Mrs. Brisbane's desk and throw that note away," I told him. He twanged in agreement.

I went right to work on unbending the paper clip. I used my paws, my teeth (ouch) and even my tiny pencil. I wiggled it, jiggled it, pushed it and pulled it. But by the time the sun came up, I was still locked in.

I'd failed Golden-Miranda, a person who would

never do anything to harm me. (The same does not apply to her dog, however.)

No wonder Mrs. Brisbane didn't give me a real job. As a classroom hamster, I deserved an F for Forgetting-to-pay-attention-to-everything-I-was-supposed-to-do!

EMPLOYMENT PICTURE BRIGHT
FOR HUMPHREYVILLE!

Students start a variety of jobs today.

𝕿he 𝕳umphreyville 𝕳erald

Miranda in Trouble

My paws were practically raw and my teeth ached from trying to remove that paper clip from my cage when I heard the doorknob turn, saw the lights come on and watched Mrs. Brisbane enter.

"Morning, fellows," she called out to us. She took off her scarf, her coat, her hat and her gloves and walked toward her desk.

Aldo's note sat squarely in the center of her desktop. It might as well have been screaming, "Read me! Read me!" I held my breath while she combed her hair, checked her face in a mirror and locked her handbag in a drawer. Then, she sat down at her desk. My whiskers drooped and my heart sank as she picked up Aldo's note and began to read.

"Oh!" she said out loud. "Oh, dear!" She studied the note for a while before walking over to my cage.

"So, Humphrey, I hear you had an adventure last night."

"Not really," I squeaked weakly.

"Squeaking will get you nowhere." She bent down and examined the lock on my cage. She tested the paper clip. "I see Aldo didn't want to take any chances."

She turned toward Og. "I suppose you witnessed the whole thing."

Og stayed motionless. Good. He wasn't going to squeal—or rather croak—on me. A true friend!

Mrs. Brisbane was staring down at my cage when Garth and A.J. arrived (they took the same bus and always arrived together), with Sayeh and Tabitha right behind them.

Mrs. Brisbane went to the door to greet the students as they bustled in and headed for the cloakroom.

Kirk came in, then Seth, then Heidi and Gail (Heidi always waited outside until Gail got to school because they were best friends).

Next Miranda came through the door, a practically perfect person who never did anything wrong on purpose and who was about to get in BIG-BIG-BIG trouble all because of me!

I wished Ms. Mac had taken me to Brazil with her.

Mrs. Brisbane went about the morning routine. First we studied the planets.

I wished I was on the planet Mars instead of in Room 26.

The teacher wrote out the words for our next spelling test. I almost fainted when she wrote the first one: TROU-BLE. Trouble was something I could spell. Trouble was what I was in. Trouble was what I had caused. My paw was shaking and I wasn't able to write all the words down. I wasn't worried about next week's spelling test. I had bigger things to worry about.

⌣•⌣

By mid-morning, Mrs. Brisbane still had not mentioned the incident from the night before. Maybe she didn't believe Aldo's note. But that couldn't be, because everybody trusted Aldo and knew he wouldn't lie.

"Og, aren't you worried about Miranda?" I squeaked when the classroom was empty at recess.

"BOING!" was his clear and obvious answer.

Of course he was worried.

I wished I was a frog in a glass house instead of a hamster in a cage with a stupid lock-that-doesn't-lock.

⌣•⌣

After recess, I was so concerned about my troubles, I hardly noticed Paul when he came in and sat down for math. My fellow classmates didn't either. I did notice him when math was over. He paused at the door and stared at the list of jobs on the board before quietly leaving the room.

Then came the moment of truth. Except it wasn't the truth. It was all a big mistake.

Mrs. Brisbane said, "Citizens of Humphreyville, please come to order." She spoke in her most serious and important voice.

"It is time to review the status of our community and the jobs you are all doing. As far as I can see, you all performed your duties as required yesterday, except for one

50

of you. I'm afraid one of you neglected your responsibility and there could have been a disastrous outcome."

My fellow classmates were clearly surprised. I glanced at Miranda's face—so totally innocent. I had to look away.

I wondered if I could go back to live at Pet-O-Rama where I came from.

"Miranda, you were in charge of Humphrey and Og yesterday." Suddenly, nice Mrs. Brisbane turned into the unsmiling Mrs. Brisbane, the way she was when I first met her.

"Yes," Miranda answered.

"Last night, Mr. Amato, the custodian, found Humphrey out of his cage. Luckily, he hadn't fallen off the table and broken his neck and Aldo put him back in the cage and locked it. It's obvious that you weren't careful when you locked his cage yesterday."

Miranda looked as sick as I felt.

"But I *did* lock the cage," said Miranda. "I remember."

"Then how do you think Humphrey got out? Do you think someone else in this class unlocked the cage?"

Miranda looked confused. "No, of course not."

"It was your responsibility. In the end, you are the one who is accountable."

Miranda was blinking hard. "I remember locking the cage," she said softly.

"YES, SHE DID!" I squeaked loudly, desperately wishing someone could understand me just this once.

"BOING!" Og chimed in.

Mrs. Brisbane ignored us. "I want you to think about how serious this is. Humphrey might have ended up stuck behind a cabinet or even gotten out in the hallway. We may have never found him again. He might even have starved to death."

My whiskers quivered and my body shivered until I remembered that I'd been out of my cage many times and none of those things had happened. In fact, I'd performed some pretty brave acts, if I do say so myself.

"In a real community, a person who doesn't do his or her job well gets fired. I'm afraid I'm going to have to fire you, Miranda."

"Oh, no!"

Mandy's hand shot up in the air and Mrs. Brisbane called on her. "You can get fired even if you're good at your job. Like if your company closes down."

"That's true, Mandy. That's different. Miranda is losing her job because she didn't fulfill her responsibilities," said the teacher. "Now, Kirk, I'll make you the Animal Keeper."

Kirk made a great roaring noise, like a lion. A few kids giggled.

Mrs. Brisbane did not giggle. She frowned at Kirk and continued. "Art, you can be the Door Monitor. Miranda, you will get no points for this job, but I will give you another chance. You can take Art's job as Energy Monitor. However, there will be consequences for your carelessness," said the teacher.

I knew Mrs. Brisbane wasn't a bad person. She was a good person, but she was doing a bad thing.

Miranda covered her face with her hands and we could all hear her crying.

"What am I supposed to do?" asked Art.

"Pay-Attention-Art," said Mrs. Brisbane, who by now was in a very bad mood. "You will be in charge of opening and closing the door at recess, lunch and the end of the day," she said. "Miranda, you may go to the restroom and wash your face."

Miranda raced out of the room, sobbing.

My heart was aching. I was afraid it was breaking. Because of me, Miranda was crying. Because of me, her grade had gone down.

I was nothing but Trouble.

Usually while my classmates eat lunch, I take a good nap. Today, I paced back and forth in my cage until Mrs. Brisbane came over. "Humphrey, let me check this lock." Thank goodness, she unfastened the paper clip, unlocked my cage, then closed it again. She tested the door to make sure that the lock was securely fastened. As usual, it seemed to be locked.

Mrs. Brisbane sighed. "I was hoping I was wrong. I was hoping the lock was broken. It's not like Miranda to forget."

"You are making an unsqueakable mistake!" I yelled.

The teacher chuckled. "Obviously you agree."

I did not!

Just then, Miranda returned. Her eyes were red from crying. "Mrs. Brisbane, I'd like to apologize," she said.

"Thank you, Miranda. But I still have to switch your job."

"I know. I'd just like to say I'm sorry to you and to Humphrey. If anything ever happened to Humphrey . . ." Her eyes filled with tears again.

"Everybody makes mistakes. Let's move on from here, okay? You go on to lunch."

Miranda nodded and went to get her lunch bag. When she returned from the cloakroom, she stopped by my cage and whispered, "I'm so sorry, Humphrey."

What Mrs. Brisbane said was true: Everybody makes mistakes. Only in this case, it was the teacher making the mistake, not Miranda. All because of ME-ME-ME.

Somehow we got through the rest of the day, although it was hard to look at Miranda, with her red eyes and her shiny nose. I saw Mandy staring at her. When it was time for afternoon recess, she hurried over to Miranda's table.

"I know that losing your job feels really bad. I'm sorry about it," she told Miranda. "Want to play tetherball with me?"

Miranda seemed surprised. She and Mandy had never been close friends, but by the time they had their coats on and were headed out the door, they were chattering away.

Art stayed in during recess to retake his spelling test. I'd been worrying about Miranda so much, I had forgotten about Art's problem. He hadn't done a good job as Energy Monitor, but Mrs. Brisbane didn't know about that. I was worried that Art had forgotten to study for his test . . . again. I had to hide in my sleeping hut so I couldn't hear Mrs. Brisbane read out the words for him. PLEASE-PLEASE-PLEASE, I thought. Please let Art pass the test!

I couldn't hear Mrs. Brisbane very well, but I certainly did hear Og when he let out a long series of BOINGs! Four or five at least. I darted out in time to see Mrs. Brisbane smile at Art. She was holding his test in her hands.

"A 95%. Art, that's the best you've done all year. Now that I know what you're capable of doing, I expect this kind of grade from now on. Think you can do it?"

Art squinched up his face. "I guess."

"Just remember to study. And pay attention, okay?"

Art nodded and got out of the classroom as fast as he could.

Whew! "Well, Og, he did it," I told my neighbor. He took a deep and splashy dive into the water of his cage, which meant he was feeling as happy about Art as I was.

Late that afternoon, Kirk took charge of Og and me. In his usual clowning way, he pretended to eat a cricket before he gave it to Og and he also made icky gagging noises when he cleaned up my poo. But he laughed, so I knew he really didn't mind.

When he was finished and the students were doing silent reading, Mrs. Brisbane quietly slipped over to my cage and checked again to see that it was locked. It was . . . or at least it seemed to be.

At last, the long and difficult day was over. I was

greatly relieved when Miranda waited until everyone had left the classroom and carefully turned off the lights.

They didn't come on again until Aldo arrived that night. "Give a cheer, 'cause Aldo's here!" he said, but I wasn't feeling too cheery. I was a tiny bit mad at him for writing that note to Mrs. Brisbane, although I knew he meant well.

"Glad to see you back in your cage," Aldo told me. "It's a dangerous world out here, you know."

After all my fur-raising adventures, I didn't need anyone to tell me that!

Aldo jiggled my cage door the way humans always do. "Nice and snug tonight," he said. "I guess Mrs. Brisbane got my note."

She got his note, all right.

I just hoped Miranda wasn't still crying.

The next morning, Miranda came bustling into the room with Sayeh and not only was she not crying, she was smiling! I guess I still have a lot to learn about human behavior. Seeing Miranda laugh made me feel a lot better. Later, though, when she passed by my cage, she looked serious again and stared at me for a few seconds.

"I'm SORRY-SORRY-SORRY!" I squeaked.

She blinked hard and turned away. For the rest of the day, she didn't cry, but she was a quieter Miranda than usual.

However, my other friends were anything but quiet.

They were so caught up in their jobs, it was hard for them to concentrate on anything else. In the middle of science, Heidi leaped up, grabbed a pencil out of Richie's hand and ran off to sharpen it. Mandy spent more time writing up "Messy Table" notices than she did labeling the planets. Mrs. Brisbane did her best to try to keep things under control.

When it was time for math, Paul slipped into class as quietly as ever. Mrs. Brisbane handed out homework papers and when he saw his grade, Art rolled his eyes and suddenly looked smaller than Paul. When Mrs. Brisbane asked if there were any questions, Miranda's hand shot up.

"It's pretty sunny outside. I was thinking that we could probably turn off the lights for a while and save some energy."

Usually, when somebody asks a question that's completely off the subject, Mrs. Brisbane isn't too happy about it. This time she smiled. "Well, I suppose we could do without lights for a little while. Thank you, Miranda. I'll add some extra points to your job evaluation for thinking of it."

Miranda acted more like her old golden self. That was good. But there was something else that was bad. At the end of the day, Art forgot to shut the door when he left. Mrs. Brisbane called him back and told him she had to deduct two points off his job score. Art was pretty upset. "Does this mean I don't get to take Humphrey home this weekend?"

Ah, so that's whose house I would be visiting on Friday night!

Mrs. Brisbane sighed and thought it over. "No, you can take Humphrey home *if* you remember to close the door every single time tomorrow."

"Gee, thanks!" Art said, carefully closing the door behind him as he left.

That night, I tried to figure out how I could fix things for Miranda. I was usually good at fixing things. I needed a Plan.

"Og, I have a brilliant idea!" I squeaked out loudly. "I'll get out of my cage tonight so Mrs. Brisbane will know that Miranda didn't make a mistake!"

"BOING!" said Og, then slid into the water and splashed wildly. I don't think he liked that idea. I thought it over some more.

"My gosh, you're right, Og! Kirk will get in trouble and I don't want that to happen. There've been enough kids in trouble this week."

I stayed in my cage the whole night. Aldo came and went, cleaning, reading and eating. Everything looked completely normal. Too bad it didn't feel that way.

HUMPHREYVILLE CITIZENS ARE REMINDED TO OBEY THE RULES
Consequences for not doing a job
are highlighted.

𝕿he 𝕳umphreyville 𝕳erald

The Difficulty with Art

On Friday, Mrs. Brisbane added up the points everyone had earned in their jobs during the first week. On the whole, my friends did well. Miranda had made up some of the points she'd lost. Heidi and Mandy lost a few points because they were overly enthusiastic about their jobs. In fact, several people weren't speaking to Mandy for handing out so many Messy Table notices, especially Tabitha, since all she had on her work space was a pile of sharpened pencils, which Heidi had put there.

"It's not fair! I was only doing my job," Mandy complained.

"A little too well," said Mrs. Brisbane in her grumpy voice.

A.J. got full points for handing out papers, Tabitha collected homework every single morning and Richie kept the plants watered, though there was an unfortunate puddle on the floor one day when he overwatered the plants.

"That plant needs a diaper," Kirk joked.

Richie cleaned the water up right away and didn't lose any points.

Near the end of the day, Mrs. Brisbane made job assignments for the next week. Seth would take care of Og and me. Heidi would erase the board while Gail would be the Energy Monitor. I could tell that Sayeh was GLAD-GLAD-GLAD to be named Mrs. Brisbane's assistant and Miranda was our new Table Inspector. No matter what her job was, she was always thinking about me. I heard her tell Seth, "Please be careful to check Humphrey's lock."

Mandy grumbled when she was assigned to water the plants, but I don't think anyone heard her except Og and me.

When class was over, Mrs. Patel arrived to pick up Art and me. She's one of our room mothers and lends a hand whenever our class needs extra help . . . or cupcakes—yum!

"I was thinking of not letting Art take Humphrey home until after our big math test next week," Mrs. Brisbane told her. "Then I had an idea. Paul Fletcher has been coming into our room for math every day because he's so far ahead of his class."

"Paul! He lives right across the street," said Mrs. Patel.

"I know. And I was thinking that maybe if the boys studied for the test together, it might help Art."

"That's a great idea," Mrs. Patel answered. "Paul hasn't been over for a long time. He and Art used to play together all the time."

"Mom, he's a whole year younger than me," Art protested. "I don't play with little kids."

"He's seven months younger than you. You used to like him a lot."

Art stood there looking miserable. "When I was a kid."

"Art, you have do something to improve your math skills," said Mrs. Brisbane. "I can recommend a tutor, if you like."

"Absolutely, let's get Art some help. He's a smart boy, you know." Mrs. Patel messed up Art's hair and he made a face.

"I know," said Mrs. Brisbane. "He's a nice boy, too."

"You know what? I think we should invite Paul over," said Mrs. Patel. "I bet he'd like to get to know Humphrey, too."

"YES-YES-YES," I squeaked. I wasn't exactly sure if Paul wanted to get to know me, but I certainly wanted to get to know him better. And maybe, just maybe, Mrs. Brisbane had a very good Plan. I like Plans a lot.

❧

We had to climb up many, many steps to get to Art's front door. Mrs. Patel wasn't much bigger than Art, so they each took one end of my cage and carried me up that way. They had trouble keeping my cage level, which meant I was sliding around like those ice skaters on Dobbs Pond, except I'll bet they were more graceful than I was. I tried to grab on to something: my ladder, my wheel, the edge of my cage. But as soon as I reached out, the cage would tilt and I'd slide in the opposite direction.

"Hang on, Humphrey. We're almost there," said Art.

I was too weak to squeak.

Somehow, we got into the house where I was set down on a table—more like *banged* down on a table—and Mrs. Patel took the blanket off my cage. "Sorry, Humphrey. We did our best." She turned to Art. "Why don't you straighten his cage out?"

Art bent down and laughed. "It looks like a tornado hit."

Mrs. Patel peered in at me with sympathetic eyes. She reminded me of Ms. Mac for a second. "Are you okay, Humphrey?"

She opened the cage door and gently took me out. This was a woman who knew how to handle hamsters. She stroked me gently with one finger while Art straightened out my bedding and put everything back where it belonged.

"I think I'll have to find a special treat for our guest," said Art's mom. "Then we'll call Paul."

Art leaned down and glumly stared at me. "Humphrey, I had a big surprise for you. We were going to have a lot of fun. Now I have to sit around and do math with Know-It-All-Paul."

"Who?" I squeaked.

"That's what some of the kids on the playground call him. Once, I think they made him cry. I guess he can't help being smart, but I wish he wouldn't ruin my weekend."

Mrs. Patel came back in with a big juicy strawberry

62

for me. "I called Paul's mom and she said he'd *love* to come over tomorrow."

Art acted as if he'd just lost his best friend. He seemed so unhappy, I couldn't even eat my strawberry. I hid it in my shavings and saved it for later.

⁛

In the evening, Mr. Patel came home from work. He was a kind man in a gray suit and he said I was a handsome gerbil. Art was paying attention for once and he told his father that I am a hamster. Mr. Patel nodded and said, "A handsome *hamster*. Do you know how to take proper care of him?"

Art showed him the guide that goes with my cage whenever I go home with students on weekends. Within minutes, Mr. Patel was reading the booklet cover to cover.

"Very interesting," he said.

A few minutes and several pages later, he added, "We must plan some stimulating activities for Humphrey."

Stimulating activities! I liked the sound of it. I jumped on my wheel and started spinning like crazy.

"He's certainly active for a nocturnal creature," Art's dad commented.

"Can I take him to my room?"

"I don't think you should move that cage around too much."

"I'll hold him." Art opened the door to my cage.

"And you won't let him get away? I understand hamsters are quick and crafty creatures." Art's dad was a pretty smart guy.

"I promise." Art picked me up and held me with both hands—gently but firmly.

"Come on, Humphrey. Wait till I show you my surprise," said Art, heading down a long hallway.

In some ways, Art's room was like most rooms I've seen. A bedroom is basically a square box with windows and a bed. Sometimes there's a desk or a dresser. Art's room had all those things. In another way, his room was unlike any room I ever imagined because just about every single inch was covered with tracks and bridges and houses and TRAINS-TRAINS-TRAINS! Not big trains but very small trains. There were open cars and passenger cars and cars I don't even know about because I'd only seen trains in pictures.

There was a big circle of track in the middle of the room with a bridge going across the middle. Inside the center of the circle was a town with houses and trees. On the edge of the town stood a red-and-white tent and a big wheel.

"What do you think, Humphrey?" Art asked as he cupped me in his hands and let me look around.

"It's unsqueakably sensational!"

"See that lake?" Art pointed to a pool of actual water near the big wheel. "That's Lake Patel."

"Blazingly brilliant!" I shouted.

"Ever since I got the train set for my birthday, it's all I can think about. I'm going to have a town and an amusement park—see, there's a Ferris wheel—and I'm going to put in a roller coaster and maybe a zoo. Isn't it great?"

"GREAT-GREAT-GREAT!" I squealed.

It *was* great. But now I knew why Art wasn't paying attention in class and why he was doodling all the time. *This* was what he was thinking about. I could see why. This world he'd created was Fun with a capital F.

Maybe this Fun was also causing Art to Fail?

Which didn't seem fair, because you should be able to have fun without failing.

Paul wasn't failing, but he didn't act like he was having a lot of fun, either.

This was all very confusing for a small hamster. But when a human has a problem, I always try my best to help, especially if that human is a friend.

Later that night, I was back in my cage and Art was back in his room, probably working on his train layout. I was spinning on my wheel when I heard Art's parents talking.

"We have to do something. His grades are falling every day," Art's mom said.

Art's dad thought for a while and replied, "I don't understand it. He's always been a bright boy. What does his teacher say?"

"She suggested a tutor. I think it's a good idea even though I'm not sure all the tutors in the world would make Art pay attention in class."

"It's that train," Art's dad said firmly. "I think we'll have to take it away from him. Once he started with that, his grades went down."

I stopped spinning. It made me SAD-SAD-SAD to think of Art losing the train set he loved so much.

Art's mom sighed. "I'd hate to, but we may have to."

The Patels sat in silence for a while. Then Art's mom said, "Paul Fletcher is coming over tomorrow. Mrs. Brisbane suggested he might help Art with his math."

"Paul? Isn't he a grade below Art?"

"Sure is. I guess he's a math whiz. He comes into Art's class for math every day."

"I hope it helps," said Art's dad. "Those two were best friends when they were little. What happened?"

"I don't know. Art seems to think Paul's too young for him to play with. But he's only seven months younger!"

The Patels both chuckled about that. Soon, they went to bed and the house was quiet.

I had all night to think of a Plan. Somehow, I had to put two and two together to get Art back on track with his math . . . and with his old friend Paul.

❧

"Look who's here," Mrs. Patel announced the next afternoon when the doorbell rang. Paul stood in the hallway, holding his math book and a notebook. "Come on, Art!"

Mrs. Patel took Paul's coat and hung it in the hall closet while she asked him how he was, how his parents were and how school was going. Finally, Art came into the room. He wasn't smiling.

"Hi, Paul."

"Hi, Art."

They stared at each other for a second. "Come say hi to our houseguest," said Mrs. Patel, leading the boys toward my cage.

66

I jumped up on my ladder and squeaked, "HI-HI-HI!"

"It's Humphrey," said Paul. He was almost smiling, I think.

"That's right. I guess you know him from coming into Room Twenty-six for math," said Mrs. Patel. "And speaking of math, why don't you boys settle in the kitchen to study? I'll fix some hot chocolate."

Neither of them moved.

"Art," said Mrs. Patel. "Take Paul to the kitchen."

Art grudgingly led Paul to the kitchen and out of my sight.

I could hear Art's mom say, "Here's your hot chocolate, guys. Now, you know how to study together?"

"I thought we could work out a few problems," Paul said.

Art didn't answer. I heard papers shuffling. I heard Paul and Art mumbling, but it was pretty clear—there wasn't all that much happening in the kitchen.

Mr. and Mrs. Patel were down in the basement. I heard her say something about "organizing the boxes."

There were occasional sounds from the kitchen. Once, when Paul made a suggestion to Art, I heard a piece of paper being crumpled up. "I don't get it. I'm not like you—some kind of genius."

Paul quietly said he wasn't a genius. He just liked math.

"I hate numbers. They're just squiggles on paper. They don't mean anything!" Art burst out.

Then things were VERY-VERY-VERY quiet.

I had my Plan, but it was risky. The last time I'd left

my cage, I'd caused some Big Trouble, especially for my friend Miranda. Still, I felt I had to take a chance in order to help Art. After all, he was my friend, too.

So I opened my good old lock-that-doesn't-lock, grabbed on to the table leg and slid down to the nice soft carpeting. I quickly darted under the table to make sure that no one was around. I could hear the boys in the kitchen and I hadn't heard Art's parents since they went down into the basement.

I took a big huge breath and scampered across the living room, turned left at the hallway and ran straight back to Art's room. Thank goodness the door was open or my Plan would have ended right then and there.

The maze of train tracks looked much different from a hamster's eye level. There were many tracks going this way and that way and a string of colorful cars attached to a big, shiny engine.

My Plan was a simple one, as most good plans are. I thought the boys would eventually find that I'd gotten out of my cage. They'd search for me and end up in Art's room. When Paul saw Art's amazing train layout, they'd start working on it together and remember how much they'd liked being friends a few years ago. Art would be willing to let Paul help him with math and his grades would go up. We'd all live happily ever after! (Except Miranda, of course. I was still feeling guilty about getting her in trouble.)

Maybe it wasn't such a simple Plan after all.

It was taking the boys a long time to discover that I

was missing. I realized it could take them hours. Or possibly, they'd never notice that I was missing at all. I yearned for my comfy cage that offered so many fun things to do, like spinning on my wheel, climbing my tree branch, swinging from my ladder or dozing in my sleeping hut.

I was feeling sleepy right then and I saw a bed that was exactly my size. It wasn't really a bed, just an open car on the train. I scurried over to it and was easily able to pull myself up the side and settle down inside. Yes, it fit me perfectly and what a thrill it was for me to be sitting in a train for the first time in my life! Ahead of me was a tank car made of gleaming metal. Ahead of that was a passenger car with tiny plastic people looking out the windows. And in front was the powerful engine with a whistle on top!

I was too excited to take a nap. Instead, I stretched my paws, and as I did, I accidentally hit some kind of switch or lever. I didn't have time to see what it was because when I touched it, the train lurched forward and began to move around the track.

Once I realized I was going on a train trip, I decided to sit back and enjoy it. I loved the way the train's wheels went clickety-clack on the track and the way it traveled in a wide curve past the general store and the tall pine trees. The train picked up speed and I could feel the breeze in my fur. Everything went dark—completely dark—for a long time. (At least it seemed long.) A tunnel! I hadn't seen that coming.

When I came out the other end, the train veered left and began to climb UP-UP-UP. I could look straight down on the roof of the general store and the tops of the tall pine trees. That Art was certainly clever to be able to build a bridge.

The train stopped climbing and moved across the straight center of the bridge. The pine trees looked small from what felt like the top of the world. But straight ahead, what I saw was Trouble! As the train started down the incline on the other side of the bridge, the bright shiny engine tumbled off the side, pulling the passenger car with its tiny people off the edge and then the shiny metal tank car. My heart skipped a beat as I realized I was headed for a huge fall, . . . and I was about to land right in the middle of Lake Patel!

HUMPHREY SPENDS WEEKEND WITH ART!
Classroom pet makes his first visit
to Patel house.

𝕿he 𝕳umphreyville 𝕳erald

Test Distress

My whole (short) life flashed before me: my days at Pet-O-Rama, Ms. Mac bringing me to Room 26, the days when Mrs. Brisbane was out to get me, the day Og arrived and the faces of all the friends I'd helped since I'd come to Longfellow School.

"Help!" I squeaked.

I heard the muffled voices of Art and Paul.

"Maybe he's in here!"

"How'd he get out of his cage?"

"I don't know . . . he just did!"

"Hurry, please!" I squeaked, because I was hanging from the bridge by one paw and I was getting TIRED-TIRED-TIRED. The cool waters of Lake Patel would have seemed inviting to Og, but hamsters are not especially fond of swimming. In fact, we're desert creatures, a fact I never knew until Richie did a report on hamsters.

"I hear him!" Art shouted.

There were sounds of footsteps as Art and Paul rushed into the room.

"Oh, no! The train fell off the bridge again," Art exclaimed.

"There he is!" said Paul. He raced forward and I dropped into his hands as gently as falling into a nice warm pile of bedding.

I must admit, I was quivering and shivering a bit, but I relaxed as Paul stroked me with his finger. "It's okay, Humphrey. You're safe now."

I looked up and saw Art staring at his train layout: the bridge, the lake, the train cars lying in a heap. "I don't understand why it always falls off. And how'd he get the train going in the first place?"

"How'd he get out of his cage?" Paul asked.

These were not questions I was about to answer.

Holding me in his hands, Paul kneeled down to inspect the train layout. "Wow, this is awesome! Did you do this all by yourself?"

"Yep." Art sounded proud. "And I have lots more I want to do."

"So that's what you're always doodling. It's really cool."

"Thanks."

"About that bridge . . . ," said Paul, handing me to Art.

"It looks okay," Art replied. "But every time, the cars tumble off the edge. Gee, Humphrey could have been hurt. The fall could have killed him. Or he could have drowned!"

"He's safe now," Paul reminded him.

"I'm a loser," Art said quietly. "I'm sorry, Humphrey."

"No problem," I squeaked softly. But it was a problem. I'd been one whisker away from plunging into—yikes—a lake! (Believe me, hamsters should NEVER-NEVER-NEVER get wet.)

Paul got down on his hands and knees, examining the bridge. "I think I see the problem."

"You do?" Art knelt down next to Paul.

"You don't have the same number of each sized support on each side. See? They look almost alike, but they're slightly different sizes."

Art did. "That's weird. It looks even."

"It's just enough to throw the train off. I'm pretty sure that's the problem if you measure them. Let's get Humphrey back in his cage and we can work on it."

"You really think you can fix it?" said Art.

"*You* can fix it," Paul replied. "It's all a matter of measurement."

"See, numbers are always my problem!" Art pretended to smack himself in the forehead.

"They aren't just squiggles on paper?"

"I get the point," Art admitted. "Can you stay awhile longer?"

"Sure. I can stay."

Luckily, when the boys put me back in my cage, they brought it into Art's room so I could watch what they were doing.

"I'll measure the supports and count them to make sure we have the same number of each." Art got out a ruler and went to work.

"We'll need two of each size," said Paul. "And I think you have a problem with this curve over here."

"I have accidents there all the time," said Art.

"The turn is too sharp for the length of the engine. We'll need to extend it," said Paul. "I'll help you figure out the angle."

I crawled into my sleeping hut for a nice long doze. I woke up when I heard a train whistle. By the time I was out of my hut, the train was climbing toward the bridge. I gulped as it chugged along the top, remembering how high it was when I'd been riding in that car.

"Keep your fingers crossed," said Paul as the train approached the downward slope of the bridge.

I must admit, though I've done some brave things in my short life, I closed my eyes. I couldn't stand the sight of that train plunging off the tracks again.

I waited for the crash but instead I heard the guys cheering. When I opened my eyes, Art and Paul were high-fiving each other. "We did it!" said Art.

"Way to go," said Paul.

Mrs. Patel appeared in the doorway, smiling. "What's going on in here?" she asked.

"Paul helped me fix the train," said Art.

"Art did all the work," said Paul.

"That's great! But how about the math?"

"We studied for a while," Paul said.

"I don't quite get it yet. Could you—I mean, would you help me some more?" Art asked Paul.

"Sure," Paul quickly replied.

"Tell you what. I'll call your mom and see if you can stay for dinner," Art's mom suggested. The boys thought it was a great idea.

"First, maybe you could clean up in here?" Mrs. Patel suggested.

Soon, Art's train layout looked neat and the extra track was put away.

"We'd better take Humphrey back to the living room," said Art, picking up my cage.

"Say, how'd he get out of that thing, anyway?" asked Paul.

"Maybe I wasn't paying attention when I closed it," said Art. "But it's not the first time. Miranda got in a lot of trouble when Humphrey got out the last time. She might not get to take him home again."

Never, ever again? My whiskers wilted when I heard that news.

Paul seemed surprised. "Miranda? That doesn't sound right. Let me check that lock."

Art put the cage down and Paul bent over and checked my cage door. I shivered a bit because Paul was one smart kid. He might actually uncover the secret of my lock-that-doesn't-lock.

"Looks fine to me," he said, and I breathed a sigh of relief.

But I only felt relieved for a while. After I was back in the living room and the boys were off studying, I wasn't thinking about trains or numbers or even the fact that I had narrowly escaped a disastrous accident.

I was thinking about Miranda and the trouble I'd caused her. Mrs. Brisbane had said there would be "consequences for her carelessness." Miranda was suffering the consequences, but the carelessness was all mine.

***

Paul ended up staying for dinner *and* spending the night *and* studying with Art on Sunday. In the afternoon, Art's dad told them he thought they needed a break and the three of them went into Art's room to work on the train layout. They were in there a LONG-LONG-LONG time. Finally, they came out with big smiles on their faces.

"Humphrey, we have a surprise for you," said Art. He opened the door to my cage.

Surprises are sometimes nice things, like birthday parties or an especially juicy strawberry. Surprises can also be scary things, like being snowed in and hungry, or strange things, like suddenly having a frog as a next-door neighbor. So as Art carefully picked me up and took me out of my cage, I had a queasy, uneasy feeling all over.

With Mr. Patel and Paul following him, Art carried me down the hallway to his room.

"It's all finished!" he said.

I peered over the edge of Art's hand. The train layout was amazing! The town now had streets and even streetlights, along with the houses and trees. Between the red-and-white tent and the big wheel were an elephant and a clown. It looked like a real town, although I could have done without the lake or the dark tunnel.

"Everything's working now," Art said. "So we thought you'd like a real train ride."

Sometimes humans imagine that they know what you're thinking. *I* was thinking I could skip riding a train ever again!

"We tested it with a weight to make sure that the car won't tip over with you in it," said Paul.

"Maybe Humphrey doesn't want a ride. Did you think of that?" asked Mr. Patel.

Art placed me in the open car. "He's the one who had the idea in the first place."

Paul pushed the switch and said, "All aboard!"

I clenched my paws along the side of the car as the train started chug-chugging down the track and around the wide curve, past the town, the general store and the tall pine trees. The train picked up speed just as it entered the tunnel. It was dark, but I didn't mind this time. In fact, I would have been happy to stay in the tunnel forever, as long as I could avoid that bridge. All too soon, it was light again and the train began its climb.

As soon as it hit the straight bridge, it picked up speed again. I tried not to look down, but I couldn't help taking a peek. Lake Patel was right below me, looking dangerously wet. At least Paul and Art and Mr. Patel were there to catch me—I hoped! All of a sudden, the train dropped and headed down the incline. I closed my eyes tightly. The speed of the train created a strong wind in my fur. When I opened my eyes, the train had almost reached the bottom of the incline and it hadn't tumbled off the tracks! I was safe.

The train veered around another curve, around the

back of Lake Patel. Whee! This was one fun ride! Suddenly, the train began to slow DOWN-DOWN-DOWN.

"Coming into the station," Paul announced.

"Don't stop now!" I squeaked. "One more time around!"

"I think he likes it," said Art. Boy, he was really paying attention now! So around I went, not once, not twice, but three more times. It was thrilling, chilling and I was perfectly willing to keep going around forever. But Art's dad said it was time to stop or I might get sick.

I must admit, when the train stopped, I felt a little strange. Once I was back in my sleeping hut, my head stopped spinning and I began to write in my notebook, trying to find the words to describe my wild ride.

A train
Makes your brain
Click and clack
Around the track.
And even when the train is slowing,
Your brain just keeps on GO-GO-GOING.

My brain kept going round and round that track all night. The next morning, when we got back to school, I couldn't wait to tell Og about my exciting adventure. But as soon as I saw Miranda come into class, I was squeakless because of that hurt look in her eyes every time she glanced at my cage.

The look that had my brain hurting.

The look that made me remember the Trouble all over again.

❧

My mind was a million miles away until it was time for math and Paul came into the room. I realized that while Art and Paul had studied hard for the test, I had not.

The test was HARD-HARD-HARD! My friends wrote and stared at their papers and stared at the ceiling, erasing and sighing. Seth sat amazingly still, glancing over at my cage now and then. Miranda did more erasing than writing, which was strange for her. Paul wrote quickly while Art seemed to struggle. He kept running his fingers through his hair, but his eyes were right on his paper.

Art was paying attention. But did he understand the math?

At last, Mrs. Brisbane called time and collected the papers. When Paul got up to leave, he whispered something to Art. Art nodded his head.

"I will mark these during lunch," said Mrs. Brisbane. "I know you're all anxious to get your grades."

When it was finally time for lunch my friends raced out of the room.

I, on the other paw, stayed inside, watching our teacher grade the papers and feeling about as worried as a hamster can feel.

Mrs. Brisbane worked quickly. Sometimes she smiled. Sometimes she frowned and made a lot of marks on the paper. Sometimes she shook her head.

I was gnawing my toes, wondering what grades my classmates were getting, especially Art.

When lunch was over and my friends were all settled, Mrs. Brisbane said, "Class, I'm not quite finished. If you'll take out your social studies books and read the chapter on how communities are organized, starting on page seventy-five, I'll keep on grading. All right with you?"

Mandy sighed loudly. Mrs. Brisbane ignored her.

"How many more do you have to grade?" Heidi asked.

"Heidi . . . what are you supposed to do before you talk?"

Heidi raised her hand.

"Thank you. I think I'll be finished by the time you've all read the chapter."

I don't have a social studies book, so I continued to watch Mrs. Brisbane and nibble at my toes. Og dove into the water for a long, splashy swim. He was probably worried about the tests, too.

Just when I thought I'd have no toes left at all, Mrs. Brisbane stood up.

"Class, I've finished grading the math papers and I'm pleased to say that all around, I've seen improvement. In fact, most of your grades have gone up."

She began to pass out the tests. One by one, I could tell what grades my friends had gotten from the expressions on their faces.

Sayeh—100%, of course.

Paul—100%, of course. Paul smiled, then glanced at Art, obviously worried about his friend.

Seth broke into a broad grin and he made a V-for-victory sign with his fingers as he turned to Tabitha. She acted happy, too.

For the most part, friends like A.J., Garth, Richie, Heidi and Gail looked relieved when they got their papers. I was holding my breath as Mrs. Brisbane handed Art his test.

"Good work," she said. "I knew you could do it."

How do I describe the look on Art's face? Glowing? Gleaming? Beaming? As happy as he looked when he viewed his beautiful train layout? All I can say is he was HAPPY-HAPPY-HAPPY and when Paul saw him smile, he beamed, too.

For once, Art had paid attention and his attention had paid off.

The only person who was extremely unhappy was Mandy. She actually put her head down on her table.

"Mandy, we can talk later," said Mrs. Brisbane.

When afternoon recess arrived, all my friends raced out of the door.

Mandy stayed behind.

Mrs. Brisbane sat down next to her. "I'm sorry, Mandy. Do you know what happened?"

Mandy lifted her head. She looked as miserable as Miranda did the day she got in trouble. "I don't know. I studied. But . . ."

She flung her head back down on the table.

Mrs. Brisbane looked sad, too. "Would you like to retake the test? I could give you another chance later in the week."

Slowly, Mandy raised her head. "If I do better, can I take Humphrey home this weekend?" she asked.

"Yes, if you can get one of your parents to sign the form."

Mandy let out a huge sigh. "I'll take the test again. And I'll get that paper signed."

"Good. Now, is there something about these problems you don't understand?"

Mandy slowly shook her head. "I just had trouble concentrating."

Mrs. Brisbane dismissed her so she could go eat her lunch.

I was too upset to eat. I hopped on my wheel and went for a spin.

MATH TEST PROVES TO BE A BIG CHALLENGE FOR HUMPHREYVILLE
"With a few exceptions, most students did well," Mrs. Brisbane reports.

The Humphreyville Herald

Double Trouble

Trouble. Rhymes with Double. Believe me, I was thinking about Double Trouble that night.

Art's good grade on the math test was cause for celebration.

Art becoming friends with Paul was cause for celebration.

Seth sitting still (or at least not popping up out of his chair every few seconds) was cause for celebration.

But I had not done one thing to help Miranda, whom I had gotten into trouble. And now Mandy clearly was having some kind of problem I didn't understand.

Lately I'd been spinning more to keep my mind off my friends' troubles. I was spinning so much, I wasn't eating all the food I had stored away in various places in my cage. (All hamsters know that it's a good idea to have some food stashed away in case of emergency.)

"Og, being a classroom pet may not be an important job, but it's not an easy one either," I squeaked to my neighbor. "Because we've got to try and keep all our friends out of trouble."

"BOING-BOING!" he twanged back at me.

He's a very wise frog.

"I'm worried about Miranda," I breathlessly told my neighbor, without stopping my wheel.

"BOING!" Og did a giant leap.

"And I'm worried about Mandy," I said.

"BOING-BOING!" Og jumped up and down twice. I knew he was worried about Mandy as well.

"And I can't think of one single thing to do that would help either one of them, can you?"

From Og: silence. This was not a good sign.

I got out my notebook and decide to make a Plan. To make a Plan, it helps to make a list. So I wrote:

PLAN TO HELP MIRANDA

1.

I stared at that *1* and stared some more. No matter how hard I stared at it, I couldn't think of anything to write. The only way I could help Miranda would be to prove to Mrs. Brisbane and the whole class that she didn't leave my door unlocked. And the only way I could prove *that* was to let everyone see that my lock-didn't-lock. Which meant that someone would put a new lock on my cage and I'd never be able to get out again. I wouldn't be able to have any more exciting adventures, and more important, it would be a lot harder for me to help my friends.

I closed my notebook and went into my sleeping hut.

I couldn't sleep because every time I closed my eyes, I saw Miranda's face in front of me.

I couldn't stand that for long, so I crawled out of my sleeping hut and went over to the side of the cage closest to Og.

"I tried to make a Plan, but I didn't get far."

Og sat there like the lumpy, bumpy frog he is and blinked his eyes.

"That is, the only Plan I can think of would mean I'd be locked in my cage forever."

Og sat as motionless as the rock he was sitting on.

"Well, you must have some ideas!" I was practically pleading with him now.

He didn't even look at me. But I'd learned an interesting fact in science class. Frogs can see all around them without moving their heads because they have 360-degree vision. That's good because they don't have much in the way of necks.

"I know you can see me, Og. And I know you can hear me, even though you don't have any ears that I can see. Are you ignoring me?"

It appeared that he was.

"Are you trying to think of a Plan, too?"

Og jumped up and let out a very loud "BOING!"

I was so startled, I jumped backward and hit my head on my wheel.

Our strange conversation—which to humans would look like a Golden Hamster squeaking and a green frog twanging—ended abruptly when the door handle rattled, the lights came on and Aldo pushed his cart into the room.

"I'm baaaack," Aldo said. His greeting didn't sound as warm and cheery as usual. In fact, he parked his cart in front of my cage and let out a loud yawn.

"Sorry, fellows. I'm kind of tired tonight. I've been studying and writing papers and working and, aw, you don't want to hear about my problems, do you?"

"YES-YES-YES!" I squeaked. Because if your friends won't listen to your problems, who will?

Aldo pulled up a chair and took out his dinner. He yawned again. "I've been working and studying more than I'm sleeping, I guess. I'm beat."

After he chewed his sandwich in silence for a few minutes, he opened his bag. "Whoa, I must be tired. I almost forgot, Humphrey. Here's a *tomahto*, thanks to Aldo *Amahto*."

It was a perfect plump cherry tomato, the kind that usually makes my whiskers wiggle with joy. But I'd been thinking so much about my problems, I didn't feel much like eating.

"Thanks," I squeaked. Aldo didn't notice that I was unusually quiet because he was yawning again.

"You know, guys, I think I'll take a short nap. I'll work twice as fast if I can just rest my eyes for a few minutes, right?"

To my amazement, Aldo rolled up his jacket, sat in a chair and, using the jacket as a pillow, put his head on the table and closed his eyes.

He was sound asleep in a matter of seconds. He really must have been tired!

It was quiet in Room 26 with only the TICK-TICK-TICK of the clock (which I couldn't hear in the daytime) counting off each second.

"Do you think he'll sleep for a long time?" I squeaked to Og. "After all, he has work to do."

Og dove into the water and went for a swim. Big help he was.

Aldo looked peaceful, dozing there. Still the hands of the clock kept moving round and round. Fifteen minutes, twenty minutes, thirty minutes. At one point, Aldo moved. Good! He was waking up! But instead, he rolled his head to the other side and kept on sleeping.

"Og, how many rooms do you think he has to clean?" I asked. After all, Aldo had a big responsibility, getting all the rooms in Longfellow School clean each night. Classrooms have a way of getting messy, with squashed crayons, crushed chalk and lots of scuff marks on the floor.

Og splashed again as he climbed back onto his rock. When I glanced over, I saw he was staring down at Aldo, too.

"I wouldn't want him to lose his job." I knew how terrible Miranda felt when she lost her job.

Og let out a big twangy "BOING!"

Aldo didn't move a muscle. He was really sound asleep.

I checked the clock. Aldo had been sleeping for one

hour! At this rate, I wasn't sure he could get his job done, at least not as well as he usually did it.

"We'd better wake him," I squeaked to Og.

I took my friend's silence to mean yes.

"On the count of three, okay, Oggy? One . . . two . . . three!"

Og and I let loose with a series of BOINGs and SQUEAKs that was quite amazing . . . even alarming! Aldo remained fast asleep. How else could one small hamster and one small frog wake up our sleeping friend?

Then I remembered something that was BAD-BAD-BAD. However, in this case, it might turn out to be GOOD-GOOD-GOOD.

Once, when I was riding the bus home with Lower-Your-Voice-A.J., Mean Martin Bean, the bus bully, told him to be quiet. When A.J. kept talking, Martin took some paper, wadded it up in a little ball and put it in his mouth to wet it. Then he threw it and hit A.J. in the neck.

"Yuck!" A.J. had said, rubbing his neck.

That wad of wet paper made an impression and gave me an idea for a Plan.

I gathered together some of my bedding material, which is shredded paper, and tried to mold it into a ball. Being a clean and sanitary hamster, I wasn't about to put the stuff in my mouth. Instead, I went to my water bottle and tapped it so a few drops trickled down onto the paper until I was able to shape it into a ball.

I worked it between my paws until it was as round and smooth as a baseball. I went to the side of my cage and looked down at Aldo, who was sleeping peacefully.

Then I had a terrible thought. I was a small hamster, after all. How could I be sure I could throw the ball so it would hit Aldo on the neck and wake him up? I'd have to throw it with all my might. Even though I was strong from spinning on my wheel and climbing ladders and tree branches, I was tiny compared to Aldo.

Then I remembered GRAVITY. Mrs. Brisbane had explained gravity to us in science. (She is an excellent teacher.) Gravity is a force that pulls things toward the ground. It's the reason we don't float above the ground all the time (which might be fun for a while, but not all the time). I realized I would have the power of gravity on my side. The ball would naturally go down. And if I aimed it correctly and put my full force behind it, I should be able to wake Aldo up.

I stopped to think about what I was doing. It was wrong for Martin to throw that spitball at A.J. Could it be wrong to do the same thing to help Aldo keep his job?

I explained my mission to Og. "I'm ready to fire on Aldo and wake him up. Do you think it's a good idea?"

"BOING-BOING-BOING-BOING-BOING!"

I think he was agreeing.

Making sure I could clear the bars on my cage, I

concentrated on a small portion of Aldo's neck and let loose.

The ball slammed downward, directly toward Aldo's neck. I crossed my paws, hoping this would work.

Bingo! That paper ball hit him square in the neck! His hand went up to rub the spot, and best of all, his eyes opened.

"Hmmm?" he mumbled sleepily.

He sat up and glanced at the clock. "*Mamma mia,* I've been asleep for an hour!"

Aldo leaped to his feet and grabbed his broom. "I thought I'd just nap for a few minutes. You guys should have woke me up! If I lose this job, I won't be able to afford to go to school."

Sometimes humans don't give credit where credit is due. But all I cared about was Aldo keeping his job.

"Whew! I'm going to have to hustle to get all my work done. I do feel better, though."

Aldo pushed his broom around the room like an artist painting a masterpiece. (We saw a great film showing a famous artist at work. I like seeing movies in class.) He missed the spitball on the floor but at least he didn't notice it. (Whew!) He finished cleaning the room in half his usual time.

"Gotta run, guys. Catch you tomorrow night!" he said as he raced out the door with his cart.

Og and I sat in silence for a while, listening to the clock TICK-TICK-TICK-ing away.

"I'm sure glad that worked," I finally squeaked.

Og jumped so high, he hit the cover of his glass house and almost popped the top.

"BOING-BOING!" he twanged.

For once, I knew exactly what he meant. Even though I'd kept Aldo out of trouble, I still had a lot more work to do.

LONGFELLOW CUSTODIAN ATTENDS LOCAL COLLEGE!

Aldo Amato says the extra hours of studying will be well worth it once he becomes a teacher.

𝕺he 𝕳umphreyville 𝕳erald

9

Too Much Payne

W hile I'd been worrying about everybody's troubles, my classmates kept working on Humphreyville. One day, they all left to go on a field trip to City Hall. How Og and I would have loved to go along! When they came back, Tabitha, Seth and Richie made a model park with swings and a slide, a baseball field and lots of trees. Tabitha must have made dozens of paper leaves for those trees!

At the same time, Richie, Gail and A.J. built a courthouse with pillars made out of the cardboard rolls that come in the middle of paper towels. (Mrs. Brisbane always keeps plenty of paper towels near my cage.)

Garth, Art and Heidi made a school out of plastic blocks. It had a playground, too! Humphreyville would certainly be a fun place to live, with two playgrounds in it.

I wasn't sure what Miranda and Sayeh were working on, but they kept looking over at me and giggling. In fact, their giggling made me uncomfortable. The more they giggled, the more I wiggled, and that made them laugh even more. I was glad to see that Miranda was feeling better.

I wished *I* felt better.

I felt especially bad when on Tuesday, Mrs. Brisbane suggested that Paul spend some time helping Mandy study for the math test she was going to retake.

"Know-It-All-Paul?" she blurted out. "He's just a baby!"

"Is not!" a voice called out.

Art had actually jumped out of his seat and his fists were clenched, though I don't think he was the type to hit anybody.

Paul looked as if someone had already punched him in the stomach.

Mrs. Brisbane wasn't happy. "Sit down, Art. Now, Mandy, that was cruel and uncalled-for. I demand that you apologize right now."

Mandy hung her head. "I'm sorry," she said. "Paul's so smart, he makes me feel dumb."

"You are not dumb, Mandy. No one in this class is dumb! Now, I want you and Paul to sit in the back of the room and go over your test together while the rest of us work on some other problems."

This time, Mandy didn't complain. She and Paul sat in the back of the room. He went over her paper and quietly talked to her about it. Sometimes she seemed puzzled. Sometimes she nodded her head. By the time math class was over, she and Paul both looked happier.

On Thursday, during morning recess, Mandy took her math test again. She worked HARD-HARD-HARD, sometimes tugging at her hair and sometimes sticking the tip of her tongue out a little. (I do that, too, when I'm concentrating.) She worked through the whole recess period and then, with a loud sigh, handed her paper to Mrs. Brisbane.

"I'll grade it right now if you like, Mandy."

"Okay, but I probably didn't do any better."

"You studied, didn't you?"

"Yes."

"Do you want to stay while I grade it?" Mrs. Brisbane asked.

"Yes, please," said Mandy.

Mrs. Brisbane took the test to her desk. Og didn't move a muscle, but I nervously gnawed on my paws. The teacher's pencil made some marks on the first page and a few on the second page. On the third page, her pencil didn't even move.

Mandy sat with her head down on the table. She couldn't stand to watch Mrs. Brisbane grade her test.

Finally, Mrs. Brisbane stood up. "You got an 85%, Mandy. That's a good solid B. Maybe even a B plus. Congratulations!"

Mandy had a smile on her face that I'd never seen before. "An 85!"

"Yes. You must have studied. And maybe Paul helped a little?"

"He did," said Mandy. "I'll thank him. And I have

something else." She reached in her pocket and pulled out a somewhat crumpled piece of paper. "The permission slip to bring Humphrey home. My dad finally signed it."

Mrs. Brisbane walked over, took the paper and examined it carefully. "Well, this is a good day for you, Mandy. Your math grade went up and you'll be taking Humphrey home this weekend. Now, you have to promise me one thing."

"What's that?" asked Mandy.

"That you'll never say you're dumb again. And that you won't ever call people names."

"I promise," said Mandy.

I felt so happy, I jumped on my wheel and spun like crazy. I heard a giant splash and knew that Og was taking a swim because he was GLAD-GLAD-GLAD, too.

For a while, I'd forgotten the Trouble. I even chowed down on some Nutri-Nibbles and yogurt drops I'd been saving. Yum!

That afternoon, Mrs. Brisbane called Miranda and Sayeh up to the front of the room. "Why don't you two tell the class about the surprise you've been working on?"

Sayeh and Miranda smiled at each other. Miranda had something wrapped in a cloth, which she set on Mrs. Brisbane's desk.

"Most communities honor the person the town is named for by putting up a statue," said Sayeh in her clear, soft voice.

"So we made a statue of our founder . . . Humphrey!"
Miranda lifted the cloth and unveiled a statue of ME-
ME-ME! It looked exactly like me except that they had
painted it shiny gold.

All the students applauded and Og let out a
loud BOING!

Miranda and Sayeh placed the statue right in the middle of the park.

"I hope you like it, Humphrey," said Miranda.

I liked it, all right. Okay, I loved it. But I didn't like
the feeling I was feeling inside. I think it's called "guilt."
It's an awful feeling, like when someone does something
nice to you but you do something rotten to her. I crawled
into my sleeping hut. The guilt feeling came right along
with me.

***

When Mandy's father arrived in Room 26 to pick us up
after school on Friday, he also had a small boy by the
hand. The boy had big brown eyes, like Mandy, and a
brown coat that was too big for him. Mrs. Brisbane
shook hands with Mr. Payne and bent down to greet
the boy.

"What's your name?"

"Bwian," he said.

"Brian? How old are you?"

Bwian—or Brian—held up three fingers.

"Three! Well, in a few years, I hope I'll have you as
a student in Room Twenty-six."

"There'll be two more coming before him," Mr.
Payne said in a gruff voice I didn't like.

Mrs. Brisbane led Mr. Payne over to my cage. "And this is Humphrey."

"I hope it doesn't eat a lot," he said, eyeing me suspiciously.

Mrs. Brisbane handed him a couple of plastic bags of food. "This will take care of him. Humphrey likes vegetable treats, too. Mandy knows what to do—right?"

Mandy nodded and tugged at her father's jacket. "Come on, Dad. Let's go now!"

"Stop rushing me."

"You left the twins in the car?" asked Mandy.

"Had to."

"Well, they'll murder each other. Come on!"

Mandy took Brian's hand and Mr. Payne took my cage. He wasn't too gentle, so I flipped and flopped around.

"Bye, Og. Wish me luck!" I squeaked to my friend. I usually feel sorry for Og. He doesn't go home with students unless it's a long weekend, because he doesn't have to eat every day.

Today, I envied him. Murder? In the car? In the car I was going to ride in?

"BOING!" Og twanged. I appreciated his concern.

It was a LONG-LONG-LONG ride to the Paynes' house, or maybe it just seemed that way because of the Payne family. In addition to Mandy and Brian, there were the twins, Pammy and Tammy. I guess they were around five years old. They may have been twins, but they didn't look alike. Pammy had light brown hair and red skin. Everything about her was round: round face, round eyes, round cheeks and a round body. Tammy was as thin as a candy cane. Her hair, eyes and skin were very pale.

There was one thing they had in common: They both liked to complain as much as Mandy did.

"I get to sit next to Humphrey," said Pammy.

"No, *I* get to sit next to Humphrey," argued Tammy.

"You're too rough," said Pammy.

"You're too loud," said Tammy.

"Pipe down!" Mandy shouted.

"You hurt my ears!" Brian complained.

"You kids all drive me crazy!" yelled Mr. Payne, glancing at the backseat.

"You're driving too fast!" said Mandy.

"He's driving too *slow*!" Tammy whined.

"You hurt my ears!" said Brian again, covering his ears with his hands.

I wanted to squeak, "PLEASE-PLEASE-PLEASE be quiet!" but no one would have heard me anyway.

Finally, we got to the Paynes' house. I figured they wouldn't argue as much outside of the car. I was wrong.

When Mr. Payne plunked my cage down on a table in the living room, it felt like an earthquake. He helped Brian take off his coat and gloves, muttering, "Hold still!"

Pammy, Tammy and Mandy threw their coats on a chair and rushed over to my cage.

"I want to hold him!" Pammy announced.

"Me first!" said Tammy.

"Later," said Mandy. She peered in at me. "Sorry about the commotion, Humphrey. I'll let you rest awhile, okay?"

"Thank you, Mandy," I squeaked loudly.

"Hear that? He said, 'You're welcome,'" Mandy told her sisters.

"I heard him say, 'You're ugly,'" said Pammy, giggling.

"I heard him say, 'I like Tammy better than Pammy,'" said Tammy, poking her twin in the ribs.

Mr. Payne slumped down in a beat-up old chair and rubbed his eyes. "Let's get this show on the road," he said. "Mandy, why don't you fix us some mac and cheese for dinner?"

"Again?" asked Mandy.

"You're the oldest."

"I hate mac and cheese," said Pammy.

"I love mac and cheese," said Tammy.

Mandy stomped into the kitchen. Brian followed her, shouting, "Bwian help! Bwian help!"

About that time, Mr. Payne turned on the television. The twins immediately raced over to watch it.

"I want Channel Five!" said Pammy.

"Channel Eleven!" said Tammy.

"Kids! Quit your bellyaching. We're watching Channel Seven and that's that," said Mr. Payne in a very firm voice.

For a while the twins were silent. The TV was loud as people screeched—or maybe they were singing. The

Paynes remained quiet until Mandy said, "Get out of the way, Brian. This is hot!"

Soon I heard Brian go "Ow!" and Mandy say, "I told you it was hot. Now sit down!"

Brian rushed back in the living room, rubbing his hand. Then he noticed me and started poking his fingers in my cage. Meanwhile, I could hear dishes banging around in the kitchen.

I sure wished I could see what she was doing. I'd been to a lot of houses and I'd never seen anyone as young as Mandy fix dinner. But that's what makes being a classroom hamster interesting: I'm always learning new things about humans.

Later, Mandy brought in plates with macaroni and cheese and the family kept watching TV while they ate. When they were all finished, they argued over who would do the dishes.

"It's your turn," said Mr. Payne.

"It's always my turn." I'd never seen Mandy so annoyed. Finally, she carried the dishes into the kitchen, muttering under her breath, "I have to do everything around here. I'll soak 'em but I won't wash 'em."

The Paynes watched TV, arguing from time to time over which channel to watch. Brian fell asleep first. Pammy fell asleep next and soon after that, Tammy dozed off. Mr. Payne carried them off to bed, one by one.

"Fun evening, huh, Humphrey?" said Mandy. She checked to make sure I had clean water and food and that my bedding was all nice and fluffy. She was really nice, although if she'd complained, I'd have understood.

"I'd like to keep you in our room, but it's too crowded," she said. "If you need anything, just squeak."

I'm never shy about squeaking up for myself.

Mr. Payne came back into the living room alone to watch TV. He dozed off eventually, but I was wide-awake. Around midnight, I heard a scritch-scratching at the front door. Mr. Payne didn't wake up and the scritch-scratching got louder. Someone was fiddling with the lock! Someone was trying to break in the house!

"Wake up, Mr. Payne! Wake up!" I squeaked as loudly as a small hamster can. Before he opened his eyes, the front door swung open, a bright light was flicked on and I heard a heavy CLOMP-CLOMP-CLOMP-ing across the floor. My eyes were adjusting to the light when a loud voice said, "What is *this* doing here!"

I saw a very tall woman looking down at me. (At least she seemed very tall to me at that moment. Most humans are tall, at least compared to me.) "How *dare* you bring this *rat* here without asking me!"

It wasn't the first time I've been insulted, but I never like being called a rat or being referred to as an "it" or a "that."

The woman didn't stop there. "If you think you're bringing another mouth to feed in this house . . . another mouth for me to support—"

"Pat, it's not like that." At last, Mr. Payne was up on his feet, rubbing his eyes. "It's Mandy's class pet and it's her turn to bring it home for the weekend."

"If the teacher wants a pet, why doesn't *she* take it home?" said Mrs. Payne. I could see her better now. She was wearing a light blue cotton top and matching pants, with white shoes. Her hair was pulled back in a ponytail and she looked tired and unhappy.

"They sent food for it. Mandy was so happy. She'll do all the work."

Mrs. Payne looked a little less angry and a lot more tired. She sighed loudly. "She'd better. Speaking of food, I'm starving."

She disappeared into the kitchen, but I could soon hear her complaining again.

"*Thank you* for washing the dishes!" I was pretty sure she was being sarcastic, because nobody actually *had* washed the dishes. "You expect me to work these awful hours at an awful place with those awful old people and come home and do the dishes?"

She was back in the living room now, yelling at Mr. Payne. "While you sit around all day waiting for a job to fall into your lap?" she continued.

"It wasn't my fault the plant closed down. You know I've been trying to find a job for a year now. I've applied everywhere."

"When was the last time you had an interview?"

Mr. Payne had that look that some of the kids get when their team loses a baseball game. "Jobs don't grow on trees. I'll do the dishes . . . *after* I fix you a sandwich."

Mrs. Payne sat down in the shabby old chair. "I know it's not your fault that I hate this job. The pay isn't even enough to support us and at night, the old people get so restless and crabby, it's awful! It wasn't as bad on the day shift, but I get paid more working at night . . . even if I hardly ever get to see my own kids."

Mr. Payne sighed. "And I see too much of them, believe me."

"I don't want to hear any complaints about the kids. They need their mother, that's all."

"You think I'm not doing a good job taking care of them?" asked Mr. Payne. His voice had an angry edge.

"You're doing an okay job. Not a great job."

Mr. Payne stomped toward the kitchen. "I'll get that sandwich. Of course, it'll just be an *okay* sandwich since I can't do anything right."

I thought Mandy's mom was about to cry. Suddenly, she noticed me again.

"What are you—a gerbil?"

"Golden hamster," I squeaked. Not that she understood—or even cared.

Mr. Payne brought his wife a sandwich and sat down on the sofa.

"More bad news," Mrs. Payne announced. "Trudy's moving to day shift, which means she can't give me a ride anymore. That means you'll have to pack up the kids in their pajamas and put them in the car—"

"I know, I know. We'll have to pick you up late at night," said Mr. Payne.

"It's not *my* fault." Mrs. Payne took a big bite out of her sandwich.

"You're saying it's my fault? Look, we've been over this a million times," he said. "I need a job and you need a break and the kids need clothes and we need another car!"

"Never mind, Jerry. Let's drop the whole thing."

Mrs. Payne nibbled at her sandwich and turned the sound up on the TV. Mr. Payne went in the kitchen and ran a lot of water, so I guess he was doing the dishes. When he came back, Mrs. Payne turned off the TV without saying a word and went to bed. Mr. Payne followed her.

Finally I was able to piece together the trouble at Mandy's house. Her father had lost his job. Her mother had a night job, apparently taking care of sick, old people, and she didn't like it. The Paynes needed more money!

All weekend, I listened to the Paynes complain to one another. But on Sunday afternoon, Mandy performed a superb cage clean for me. First, she put on the throwaway plastic gloves Mrs. Brisbane made all the kids use. She took a plastic spoon and cleaned up my poo corner, fluffed up my bedding, and changed my water dish, and while she did, she talked to me. Now I was only too happy to listen.

"I'll bet the other houses you go to are happy and fun and everybody laughs all the time—right? We used to be like that. Well, kind of like that, till Dad lost his job. You understand?"

I squeaked as sympathetically as I could.

"I'm glad you can't talk. I wouldn't want you to tell my friends about my awful family."

"They're not awful." I had to squeak up. In truth, they were pretty awful, but more than that, they were unhappy.

Just then, her mom came into the room. It was Sunday, but she was dressed to go to work. "What on earth are you doing?" she asked.

"Cleaning Humphrey's cage," Mandy explained.

"That's disgusting! I can't believe your teacher makes you do that kind of stuff. It's worse than my job and you don't even get paid for it!"

"Really, it's okay," said Mandy. "I have gloves, see? I put everything in a plastic bag. I don't mind."

"Well, I do." Mrs. Payne looked around the room. "Where is your father?"

"How should I know?"

I wasn't sorry when Mrs. Payne tromped out of the room. I *was* sorry she was so unhappy.

"Lucky you, Humphrey. You don't have to live here all the time," said Mandy as she closed my cage and ripped off her gloves. She even jiggled the lock to make sure I couldn't get out.

"Gotta go wash my hands. Back in a flash."

While Mandy was gone, I thought about all the students and their families I'd helped on my weekends visiting. I'd managed to get Miranda and her stepsister to go from being enemies to being friends. I'd helped Principal Morales, the Most Important Person at Longfellow School, get his children under control. I'd even helped our teacher's husband, Mr. Brisbane. Still, what could one small hamster do to help with such a BIG-BIG-BIG problem?

This family was in trouble and I didn't have any idea of how to help.

I knew one thing: Compared to the Paynes, I had absolutely nothing to complain about.

HUMPHREY SPENDS WEEKEND
WITH THE PAYNES
"I've dreamed of this for a long time," says Mandy.

𝕿he 𝕳umphreyville 𝕳erald

My Payne-full Problem

umphreyville is going to have some special visitors in two weeks," Mrs. Brisbane announced as soon as class began on Monday.

There was a buzz around the classroom. Who would these guests be?

"We're having a Parents' Night so your families can see what a great town you've created. And I've invited one of our City Council representatives to come talk about our own community."

A City Council representative sounded Very Important. Almost as Important as Principal Morales.

"We'll have to make sure that Humphreyville is in the best shape possible in the next two weeks."

All my friends were excited. Mrs. Brisbane gave out new job assignments for the week. When Gail was named Animal Keeper, I couldn't help noticing that Miranda stared down unhappily at her table. How could one small hamster (namely me) have caused trouble for one nice human (namely Miranda)?

Suddenly, Mandy began to wave her hand. Mrs. Brisbane called on her.

"I think it's unfair," she said in her cranky voice.

"What is unfair?" asked the teacher.

"Paul doesn't have a job. He's part of our class, too, and he's helped us with our math. Well, me at least. Why can't he have a job?"

For once I agreed with Mandy's complaint, and so did Art.

"He helped me, too," he said. "And he always checks that list of jobs."

I had to speak up, too. "They're RIGHT-RIGHT-RIGHT!"

"I agree!" Mrs. Brisbane replied. "I don't know why I didn't think of it. And I know the perfect job for him, too. He can be the Class Accountant and add up all these points you're earning."

Mandy bounced up and down in her chair. "Can I tell him?"

"No, let me!" Art protested.

Mrs. Brisbane laughed and shook her head. "You can *both* tell him."

At the end of math class, they did.

Paul looked so tall when he left the room, he must have been walking on air.

That night I waited anxiously for Aldo to come in. I was prepared to do anything to keep him awake. In fact, Og and I decided to practice louder wake-up calls in case Aldo was sleepy again. I was SQUEAK-SQUEAK-

SQUEAK-ing, Og was BOING-BOING-BOING-ing and the crickets were chirping in the background when the custodian entered.

"Whoa, fellows, why all the noise?"

Og and I quickly quieted down, but the crickets kept singing away.

Aldo was his old peppy self again as he wheeled in his cart and spun it around. "I feel like making noise, too, because I'm not tired tonight. Nosiree. I came armed with this!"

He reached down on a shelf of the cart next to his lunch bag and held up a metal container. "Maria made me a big thermos of coffee. It will keep me awake until I'm finished cleaning."

"GOOD-GOOD-GOOD," I said, and when he opened the thermos, the coffee smelled yummy, even though it isn't something hamsters usually drink. I was glad I didn't have to launch another unsanitary spitball that night.

The next morning, it was pouring rain. March was still coming in like a lion, just like Seth's grandma Dot had said. When Mrs. Brisbane took attendance, no one answered when she called, "Mandy Payne," "Art Patel" or "Heidi Hopper." None of them had shown up for school!

From time to time, one of my fellow students missed a class or two because of the sniffles or a cough, but on the whole, we had a healthy class and this was the first time three students were sick at the same time.

Mrs. Brisbane made sure that the Homework Monitor, who was A.J., wrote down all the assignments to send home to them.

I spent most of the morning watching the rain drip down the windows, making everything outside—the trees, the street, the passing cars—look blurry. It was too wet for my friends to go outside for recess, so they stayed inside and worked on Humphreyville.

When lunchtime came, my friends raced out of class as usual. Mrs. Brisbane was preparing to go to lunch herself when Mr. Morales entered. He was wearing a tie that had all the letters of the alphabet on it in bright colors.

"Sue, can you talk for a minute?" he asked. Sue is Mrs. Brisbane's first name. Most students don't even know their teachers have first names.

"Of course. Have a seat," Mrs. Brisbane told him.

"I don't want to take up too much of your time, but I have to tell you, I've had a complaint from a parent."

Mrs. Brisbane was surprised. "Who's that?"

"Mrs. Payne. Apparently Mandy and her whole family are sick. Coughs, runny noses, watery eyes. And she blames it all on . . . Humphrey."

Blames . . . me? I felt as if all the air was being sucked out of me.

Mrs. Brisbane was as surprised as I was. "Humphrey! Why on earth would she think that?"

"Well, he spent the weekend at their house and now they're all sick."

"So are Art and Heidi . . . and the weather has been

horrible. Goodness, I think I've had *fewer* absences this winter than usual."

"I believe you, but she's pretty angry. She doesn't think the kids should have to clean his dirty cage. She's called some of the other parents. She even threatened to start a petition to get all classroom pets banned!"

Banned! My whiskers drooped and my heart was heavy.

"BOING!" Og burst out. I guess he realized he was a classroom pet, too.

"That's ridiculous. Just because her children have colds . . ."

"Mrs. Payne says her children are never sick. She said she's going to the school board and expects all their medical costs to be paid."

Now Mrs. Brisbane was getting angry. "Paid by whom . . . Humphrey? You've had him in your house. I've had him in my house. We didn't get sick."

"I'm on your side, but I have to respond to her. I'll compare the attendance records from last year to this year to see if there's any difference. You could check to see if any of the other students have gotten sick after Humphrey's been at their houses. And I'll talk to the other teachers who have classroom pets."

"Yes, those guinea pigs in Room Fourteen," said Mrs. Brisbane. "And the frog in Angie Loomis's class. And there are rabbits in Mr. Olinsky's class. Oh, but the children love to have Humphrey come home with them! The parents love him, too."

"Except for the Paynes."

Mrs. Brisbane got very quiet. She was thinking of something. And I don't think it was something good.

"Art Patel is absent today and he had Humphrey at his house last weekend. I'll call his mother and see what's wrong with him."

"Good idea. And for now . . ." Principal Morales stopped and glanced over at Og and me. "Maybe you'd better keep Humphrey at your house. Og, too. Mrs. Payne was pretty upset. She even said she might call a lawyer."

A lawyer! Was I going to end up in court? Or in jail?

This wasn't just Trouble with a capital T.

This was TOTAL DISASTER with a capital everything!

For the rest of the day, I stared through the bars of my cage and imagined myself looking through another set of bars: the bars on a jail cell. Would Og end up in there with me, too? After all, he was a classroom pet, although he didn't go home with students on the weekend.

At the end of the day, Principal Morales helped Mrs. Brisbane cover my cage and carry Og and me out to the car. Thank goodness the rain had stopped. They brought along our food, including Og's icky, yucky crickets. Luckily it was cold, so they were quiet in the car.

"I'm really sorry about this, Sue," the principal told Mrs. Brisbane through the car window.

"My husband will be thrilled to have these two home with him. But I'm afraid my students will be very disappointed."

VERY-VERY-VERY, I thought.

"I'll try to get this resolved as soon as possible," Mr. Morales promised.

Mrs. Brisbane thanked him and rolled up the window. Soon, we were on our way to her house—but for how long?

Just as she'd said, Mr. Brisbane was really glad to see us. Mrs. Brisbane honked the horn and he came out to the driveway in his wheelchair to meet her, even though it was extremely cold.

"Put Humphrey's cage right here across the armrests," he told his wife. "I'll come back and get Og."

"Okay. I'll bring in the food."

Soon, Og and I were side by side on the Brisbanes' wide coffee table. It was warm and cozy in their house, and before long, Mr. Brisbane had everything in my cage and Og's house in tip-top shape. Mrs. Brisbane came in with steaming cups of tea and the two of them sat and watched us as they drank it.

"This Payne family sounds like a nuisance," said Mr. Brisbane.

"I don't know much about them. Mandy complains a lot, but she's a nice girl. I think it's a habit she's picked up."

"Maybe she has a lot to complain about," Mr. Brisbane said.

"YES-YES-YES!" I said, hopping on my wheel and spinning to get their attention.

"Whatever their problems are, they don't have to take them out on Humphrey, do they, buddy?" Mr. Brisbane wiggled a finger through the bars of my cage.

Mrs. Brisbane picked up the phone and called Art's mother.

"I'm checking to see how Art is doing," I heard her say. "We missed him in school."

I would have loved to hear what Mrs. Patel was saying. Mrs. Brisbane said, "Oh," and "I'm sorry," and "What did the doctor say?" She listened and then said, "Did Art show any signs of illness right after Humphrey was there?"

I held my breath while she waited for Mrs. Patel to answer.

"This is private, but since you're a room mother, I'll tell you that a parent has complained that having Humphrey at her house made her whole family sick. He and Og are temporarily banned from the classroom."

Art's mom answered so loudly, even I could hear her say, "That's ridiculous!"

"I know, Mrs. Patel, but we have to check this out. No, I can't tell you who it is. A number of students were absent today. I'll let you know. And I think you should keep Art home another day."

After a polite good-bye, Mrs. Brisbane hung up and turned to her husband.

"He has a bad cold. Her husband got it first. Every-one in his office has had it."

"Well, they didn't catch it from Humphrey," Mr. Bris-bane said, setting his cup down hard.

"No. She was terribly upset. You can imagine how the children will feel. I'll call the Hoppers."

After a short talk with Heidi's mother, Mrs. Brisbane told her husband that Heidi also had a bad cold, but that she had gotten soaked in the rain two days before.

"Humphrey had nothing to do with that. He hasn't even been to her house," Mr. Brisbane insisted.

"You know, I think I'll make another call . . . to the Paynes."

"The Paynes! I wouldn't talk to that pack of trouble-makers."

"Now, Bert. You can catch more flies with honey than with vinegar, you know."

Sometimes humans say the strangest things. Why was she calling the Paynes about catching flies? Og might be interested, but not me!

"That is a silly expression, if you don't mind me say-ing so, dear," said Mr. Brisbane.

Mrs. Brisbane laughed. "You're right. I've never un-derstood why anyone would want to catch flies."

"Except a baseball outfielder." Bert laughed at this joke and so did his wife, although I didn't understand it at all. Of course, I'd never been to a baseball game.

Before I could figure it out, Mrs. Brisbane decided to call the Paynes. I held my breath again while she waited for someone to pick up. "Hello, is this Mr. Payne? This is Mrs. Brisbane, Mandy's teacher. How is Mandy feeling?"

She and Mr. Payne had a long exchange about Mandy's health and the health of Tammy, Pammy and Brian. Then she said, "Well, I certainly hope Mandy will be back in the classroom soon. We all miss her."

She paused to listen for a while longer. "The animals are home with me and we're looking into it. Please give Mandy my best. By the way, is Mrs. Payne there? I'd like to talk to her."

Mr. Payne gave a short answer this time. "I see. Well, please tell her I called. Thank you. Good-bye."

Mrs. Brisbane hung up the phone and took a long sip of tea.

"What did he say?" Mr. Brisbane was not a patient man. At that moment, I was not a very patient hamster.

"It sounds as if they all have colds, like Art. When I asked about Mrs. Payne, I learned something new. Mrs. Payne works at night."

"That could be hard on the family," said Mr. Brisbane.

I had to squeak up. "It IS-IS-IS! Especially since Mr. Payne lost his job."

Mr. and Mrs. Brisbane burst out laughing. "I think Humphrey is trying to tell us something."

Mrs. Brisbane became more serious. "I wish we could understand him. After all, he spent a whole weekend there. I'll bet he could tell us a lot."

116

Boy, was she right. I could write a book about the Paynes! (If I only had room left in my notebook.)

It was pleasant at the Brisbanes' house. They took me out of my cage and made a maze for me to run on the floor, but my heart wasn't in it. About the second time around, the phone rang and Mrs. Brisbane answered.

"Aldo! Is everything all right?"

She listened for a few seconds, then replied, "Sorry. I should have left a note for you. Of course you'd be worried. No, I have Humphrey and Og here for a while. Frankly, there was a complaint about Humphrey making one of the students sick, but please don't tell anyone, not even Richie's family. I don't know how long they'll be here." She laughed. "I will definitely give them your regards."

Once she hung up, Mrs. Brisbane told Og and me that Aldo missed us.

"How did he happen to have our number?" Mr. Brisbane asked.

"I gave it to him when he was trying to decide to go back to school, in case he had any questions. He's going to make a great teacher."

Yes, Aldo would make a great teacher unless he fell asleep on the job. And now I wasn't there to wake him up if he was tired. I hoped he had a lot of coffee with him.

When she was ready to go to bed, Mrs. Brisbane brought me a slice of apple, but it didn't appeal to me.

"I'm not hungry, are you, Og?" I asked my friend a little later.

"BOING!" he answered.

For the rest of the night he was quiet. The crickets were quiet. I was quiet, too. My brain wasn't quiet, though, as I thought about the next day, when I would be absent from class for the very first time.

<hr>

It felt so strange to see Mrs. Brisbane head off for school. I couldn't imagine Room 26 without me. I could imagine it without Og, since I was there before he was. But I'd never seen Room 26 without me in it. How could I?

As the day went on, I tried to picture my classmates having math class, doing their school jobs, working on Humphreyville—named for me!

Mr. Brisbane tried to keep my mind off school by giving my cage a terrifically good clean, though he did uncover a secret.

"Humphrey . . . I don't think you've been eating your food. You've just been hiding it!"

I hung my head because it was true. Ever since Miranda got in trouble, I hadn't been hungry. My yummy treats didn't taste yummy anymore.

"If you don't eat, you'll get sick," said Mr. Brisbane. "Now, I'm going to give you some yogurt drops right now and you're going to eat them."

"Yes, sir," I squeaked weakly.

Mr. Brisbane headed his wheelchair for the kitchen,

then abruptly stopped. "Wait a second. Maybe you *are* sick! Why didn't I think of this sooner? You need to see a veterinarian!"

I was puzzled, trying to figure out why a veterinarian could help. I'm practically a veterinarian myself because I only eat fruits and nuts and vegetables. (I have heard of hamsters who like a bit of meat on occasion!)

Soon, Mr. Brisbane whizzed back into the room with some crunchy, munchy yogurt drops. "Eat up, my boy. You have to keep your strength up. You can't give in to troubles. You have to fight back!"

Was that really what I was doing? Giving in to troubles like Mr. Brisbane had done the first time I met him?

I reached down and took a yogurt drop and ate it. It tasted good. I realized I was hungry, so I took another one.

"That's a good fellow. You've got plenty of fight left in you, haven't you?"

A few more yogurt drops and I felt a little fight coming back.

"I'll call the neighbors to get the name of their vet and I'll make you an appointment. You'll be back in the classroom before you know it."

Mr. Brisbane seemed determined, but Mrs. Payne was determined, too.

Once Mr. Brisbane went off to make his calls, I asked Og, "Don't you miss school, old pal?"

The frog who usually sat like a large green lump began to jump up and down, twanging loudly. "BOING-BOING-BOING-BOING-BOING!"

I took that to be a yes.

HUMPHREY AND OG MISSING
FROM ROOM 26

Mrs. Brisbane says they are safe at her house; no explanation for their absence is given.

𝕿he 𝕳umphreyville 𝕳erald

The Difficulty with Dr. Drew

It turns out I was confused.

A *vegetarian* eats only vegetables.

A *veterinarian* is an animal doctor. Not a doctor who is an animal, but a human doctor who takes care of animals, like dogs, cats, horses and hamsters. Sick hamsters.

Mr. Brisbane was right. I hadn't been eating much lately, but it wasn't because I was sick. It was because I felt so guilty about Miranda. Could a veterinarian (Mr. Brisbane called it a "vet") figure that out? I didn't think so.

It was quiet in the Brisbanes' house for most of the day. Mr. Brisbane spent a lot of time in his workshop making things out of wood, like birdhouses and picture frames. Og was unusually quiet, even for him. There were no giggling students or recess bells or spelling tests to keep me awake. I finally crawled into my sleeping hut, but I didn't actually fall asleep. I kept picturing my friends hard at work on Humphreyville. Or since I was

121

in so much trouble, maybe they'd changed the name. Somehow, "Ogburg" didn't sound very good to me.

Time dragged on until Mrs. Brisbane finally came home.

"How are the guys?" she asked her husband.

"Fine, fine, although Humphrey is quieter than usual. Did you get my message about the vet?"

"Yes. I telephoned Mrs. Payne to tell her we're getting Humphrey examined this afternoon. In fact, I invited her to come along."

Gulp. I was going to the vet's office that same afternoon? With Mrs. Payne?

"What did she say?"

"She goes to work at four o'clock." Mrs. Brisbane checked her watch. "Which reminds me, we'd better get going if we're going to make it there by four-thirty."

Four-thirty? It was close to four-thirty already. I only had time to squeak, "Wish me luck," to Og before my cage was covered and I was whisked out the door with the Brisbanes.

As long as I'd been in Room 26, I'd worried about the problems of my classmates.

Now I was in Big Trouble myself . . . and my friends didn't even know about it!

❧

I was glad my cage was covered because the air was freezing cold. But traveling that way is like being blind-folded. By the time I could see what was going on around me, I was in the waiting room of the veterinarian's office.

"Dr. Drew will see Humphrey in a few minutes," a man behind a desk told us.

I had a few minutes to look around and I was SHOCKED-SHOCKED-SHOCKED!

To the right of me was a large white dog with brown freckles and huge teeth, like Miranda's unfriendly dog, Clem. He licked his chops. That meant he was hungry!

I quickly turned my head. To the left of me was a cage with a cat in it. The cat had black fur and white paws. Its dark green eyes were staring right at me, a little *too hard* for my own comfort.

I decided to look straight ahead, where there was a huge tank with fish of every color. Some had stripes and even polka dots, and they swam round and round a pink castle. I wished I could be behind glass instead of sitting so close to those two dangerous creatures. Those "few minutes" the man at the desk had mentioned seemed like a few hours to me.

Then something shocking happened. The door swung open and in walked Mr. Payne, followed by Mandy, Pammy, Tammy and Bwian. I mean Brian.

Mrs. Brisbane was as stunned as I was. "Mandy! What are you doing here?"

Mandy looked as if she wanted to be anywhere but in that office. Mrs. Brisbane gained control of herself and put her hand out to Mr. Payne. "Hello, Mr. Payne. This *is* a surprise." She introduced the Paynes to Mr. Brisbane and everyone said hello. I must say, Mr. Payne didn't seem very happy to be there. Mandy acted even unhappier. (I didn't know if that was because of me or because of her red nose.) Pammy and Tammy were too busy kicking each other to notice where they were, while Brian tore pages out of a magazine.

"The wife said I should come and see what the doc says." Mr. Payne was extremely glum. "If that's okay with you."

Mrs. Brisbane politely said it was fine with her, but it didn't seem fine to me. Mandy's mom didn't trust Mrs. Brisbane to tell her honestly what the doctor said? *That* ruffled my fur a bit.

"Now see here, Mr. Payne," I squeaked, which wasn't such a good idea. When they heard me, the dog and the cat got excited, barking and snarling and growling and meowing in a very unnecessary way! I only hoped they wouldn't discover that my cage had a lock-that-doesn't-lock.

Just as I was about to escape into my sleeping hut for safety, a woman dressed all in pale green entered. She had dark skin, dark hair and big, dark eyes, like Ms. Mac, my first teacher.

"Hi, I'm Dr. Melissa Drew. Is Humphrey all set?"

I was all set to get out of that waiting room, I can tell you that!

Mrs. Brisbane stepped forward and introduced everyone to the vet. It was decided that Mandy and her sisters and brother would stay in the waiting room while the adults came into the examination room with me.

It was nice and warm inside, so why was I quivering and shivering?

Dr. Drew put my cage on a padded table and smiled at me. "Now, Humphrey, is this your first exam?"

"YES-YES-YES!" I squeaked loudly, which made Dr. Drew smile even more.

"He certainly sounds healthy," she said as she opened my cage, reached in and took me out. "Don't worry, Humphrey. This won't hurt a bit."

Dr. Drew spoke to the humans. "This isn't any different than the kind of examinations you get. Now, has Humphrey had any problems lately?"

"He's pretty peppy, but he hasn't been eating as much as usual," said Mr. Brisbane.

"Made all my kids sick," said Mr. Payne.

Dr. Drew was surprised. "Really?"

"Yep. He spent the weekend at our house and all my kids got sick. Some of the other kids at school, too. Right?" He turned to Mrs. Brisbane.

"Everyone who's been sick seems to have a cold, even children who didn't take Humphrey home," Mrs. Brisbane said firmly.

"It's highly unusual for humans to get sick from handling a hamster. It's more common for a hamster to pick up a disease from a human or another animal. But let's check him out."

Dr. Drew's touch was so gentle, I relaxed. She put one hand underneath me and held her other hand above my head, making a little tent for me. VERY-VERY-VERY nice.

"We'll check the eyes first, because that's where we

usually see signs of infection or disease in hamsters." Cupping me in one hand, she shined a tiny light directly in one eye. Whoa—that's a wake-up call. Next, she checked my other eye.

"Looking good," she said. "No discharge or inflammation. Now I'll listen to his heartbeat."

Dr. Drew picked up a stethoscope (a word I do *not* want to see on a spelling test). It had a plug for each of her ears and a teeny piece that she held against my chest. First, she listened. Then, she smiled. "Excellent. A very healthy heart, Humphrey. Now let's check out that weight."

She set me on a scale that was flat and square. She also put a few chunks of Nutri-Nibbles on the scale. "Those will keep him there for a second." She let go of me and while I picked up a treat, she said, "Well, even if he's not been eating well, his weight is completely normal."

While I nibbled away, Dr. Drew and Mrs. Brisbane discussed what I ate.

"He usually eats everything: vegetables, fruit, hamster food, yogurt drops," Mrs. Brisbane said.

"Excellent," said the vet. "Lots of variety. That's what hamsters like—right, Humphrey?"

"You bet!" I squeaked, and the doctor chuckled.

"But I just found some old food hidden in his cage and realized he's not been eating as much as before," Mr. Brisbane said.

Dr. Drew bit her lip for a second, then asked, "Has there been any change in his environment lately?"

Mrs. Brisbane nodded. "Well, I had to take him out of the classroom because of the complaint."

I noticed Mr. Payne was staring at his shoes.

"So I guess things are a little upset for him," my teacher added.

"That could be it," said Dr. Drew. "Some hamsters are very sensitive even to small changes."

She was right about that. I am a very sensitive hamster. And Dr. Drew is a very good veterinarian.

"Sometimes hamsters get infections in their cheek pouches because they store food there. So, open wide, Humphrey." She picked me up and gently pulled my mouth open, using the small light to look inside. "Clean as a whistle," she said. "Fur is nice and shiny. I'll take a sample of some stool, if there's any in there."

I was confused, but it turns out that stool is poo. She took some from my cage with a tweezers and put it in a tube.

"It's nice and firm, which is a good sign."

What a surprise! Usually when my classmates clean my cage, they go, "Ewwww" or "Yuck" when they get to the poo part. But it didn't bother the doctor at all. She even had a nice name for it: stool.

The vet held me up to her eye level and said, "Humphrey, we need to get you back to your old environment, but in the meantime, you are one healthy, handsome hamster."

I remember when Ms. Mac picked me out at Pet-O-Rama and told Carl, the store clerk, "He's obviously the most intelligent and handsome hamster you have." I sure missed Ms. Mac, but she sent me postcards, so I knew she still cared. Dr. Drew cared, too. She may not have been able to figure out that I felt guilty about Miranda, but she had figured out that I wasn't sick.

"Try varying his food even more. And just to make sure he perks up, I'm giving you some yummy vitamin chews. I guarantee Humphrey will like them."

I liked them already. In fact, I felt so happy, I was a little hungry.

She gently put me back in my cage. "Humphrey, I have a friend here today you might like to meet." She went to the door and called out, "Judy? Could you bring Winky in here?"

Then she turned to Mr. Payne. "Tell me, what did the doctor say about your children's illnesses?"

Mr. Payne looked down at the tips of his toes and squirmed like Sit-Still-Seth.

"Didn't take them. Kind of expensive. See, we haven't got insurance, and . . ."

"I see," said the vet. "But they're better now."

"Yes. They had runny noses and coughs and a temperature for a few days. Just about drove me nuts. I take care of them now that I . . ." He stopped. Mr. Payne sure had a hard time finishing sentences.

"Well, I don't think it was from Humphrey," said the vet.

"The wife's convinced it is."

There was silence until Mrs. Brisbane said, "Dr. Drew, could you write a report or a letter and send it to Mrs. Payne? That would probably put her mind at ease.

128

In fact, I could pass it on to the principal and other parents."

Dr. Drew smiled. "Sure! I'd be glad to."

Just then, the door opened and a blond woman who wore a pink smock with pictures of teddy bears all over it came in, carrying a small cage. "Here's Winky," she said.

Dr. Drew introduced everyone to Judy and said, "Judy rescues hamsters. Sometimes she has more than twenty of them in her house."

"Rescues them from where?" asked Mr. Brisbane. It was the exact question I wanted to ask. I was picturing hamsters on top of burning buildings . . . floating down rafts in a flood . . . trapped by the weight of an avalanche!

"Sometimes people decide that taking care of a hamster is too much work. That's something to think about when you get a pet," said Judy. "Mostly I get them from Pet-O-Rama. They're rejects, like Winky here."

"Reject hamsters?" asked Mr. Brisbane.

"Yes, if they're not perfect, people won't buy them." She put Winky's cage on the table next to mine. I could easily see how he got his name because he was winking at me. I winked back.

"For some reason, Winky was born with one eye and he doesn't have any teeth. Neither of those things bother him. He's able to eat a variety of foods and he only needs one good eye."

"He does look like he's winking," said Mrs. Brisbane. "He's very cute."

He was not as handsome as I am, but I have to admit, he looked like a nice fellow.

"Hi, Winky. You look fine to me," I squeaked.

And was I surprised when he squeaked back. "Thanks, fellow. I was kind of worried when Pet-O-Rama rejected me. Luckily, Judy came around and rescued me."

He understood me and I understood him. This was a first!

"Pet-O-Rama! That's where I came from!" I told him.

"Remember Carl? He just got made assistant manager," Winky squeaked at me.

"Imagine that!"

"They had a big party to celebrate," he added.

"You don't say. Hey, did they ever sell that chinchilla?" I asked.

"Yep. A real nice family took him," he told me. "Oh, and just before I left, they got in a big shipment of new hamster cages. One of them is four levels high."

"No kidding!"

Suddenly all the humans, even Mr. Payne, were laughing.

"Sounds like these two have a lot in common," said Mrs. Brisbane.

"Let's get them a little closer." Dr. Drew took me out of the cage again. Judy took Winky out of his cage.

"Now, you shouldn't put hamsters together in the same cage unless they've been raised together. But they can sniff each other."

Judy held Winky up close to me and we stared at each other, eye to eye. I took a big sniff. Yep, he was a hamster all right.

"Where do you live now?" he asked.

"In a school room with lots of kids," I said.

"Sounds like fun," Winky replied.

"It is. But it's work, too."

Winky definitely winked at me. "Nice work if you can get it, pal."

With that, we were whisked back into our cages.

"If you know anyone who wants a special, winking, happy hamster, give me a call," said Judy.

I only had time to squeak, "Good luck," before Winky was gone.

"Any other questions?" asked the vet.

No one had any, so my cage was closed up and we were ready to go. Before we got to the door, Dr. Drew said, "Oh, by the way, if you know anyone searching for a job, we have an opening for a veterinary assistant."

Mr. Payne stopped in his tracks. "What's that?"

"Someone to feed the animals, give them water, take them for walks, clean their cages, give them medicine. The person has to be able to lift heavy bags of food, interact with animals, that sort of thing. We'll train."

Mr. Payne had a strange look in his eyes. "And the hours?"

"There's some flexibility there. Do you have someone in mind?"

Mr. Payne hesitated. I decided to squeak up for him.

131

"He needs a job! Hire Mr. Payne! PLEASE-PLEASE-PLEASE!"

Dr. Drew turned toward me. "Humphrey, do *you* have someone in mind?"

"MR. PAYNE!" I never squeaked so loudly in my whole life.

"I know you're trying to tell us something."

Mr. Payne cleared his throat. "I might be interested. I mean, I don't know if I'm right for the job."

The vet turned to him and smiled. "How do you feel about taking care of animals?"

"Good," Mr. Payne said. "I had a nice dog when I was a kid. Name was Lady. And I learned a lot from watching this exam. I'm strong. I'm a good worker."

"Why don't you fill out an application now and come in and talk to my partners and me tomorrow morning? You can bring the children if you need to."

I saw something new in Mr. Payne's eyes. They came to life for a few seconds.

"Okay," he said.

Soon we were out in the waiting room. Mandy was holding a funny dog in her lap. He had short legs and a long body. Tammy, Pammy and Brian stood around her, staring at the odd animal.

"See, Dad? It's a wiener dog!" she cried out.

The lady sitting next to Mandy, who obviously owned the dog, smiled. "A dachshund, actually. His name is Fritz."

Fritz did look like a wiener. Or a sausage. Or a hot dog.

132

"Do you like dogs, Mandy?" asked Mrs. Brisbane.

"Yes. And cats, too. But what I'd really like is a hamster."

Smart girl, that Mandy.

Dr. Drew took Fritz and his owner into the office.

"Kids, I've got to fill out some papers," said Mr. Payne. "Please be quiet and let me concentrate."

"Okay. We'll watch the fish," said Mandy. "How's Humphrey?"

"Humphrey?" said Mrs. Brisbane. "Humphrey is just perfect."

It was nice to hear that I was perfect, even though I knew I was not.

HUMPHREY EXAMINED BY VETERINARIAN

Students anxiously await
classroom hamster's medical report.

𝕿he 𝕳umphreyville 𝕳erald

The Domino Decision

I was hoping to get back to school the next day, but Mrs. Brisbane said she wanted to present the doctor's report to Principal Morales and Mrs. Payne and the room mothers so that everyone would agree that it was all right for me to go back in the classroom. That was disappointing, of course. For one thing, my friends were putting the finishing touches on Humphreyville. For another thing, Og got to go back to Room 26—since nobody accused him of making humans sick—and I was all alone at the Brisbanes' house.

The Brisbanes were nice, but my job was to help my classmates and it was pretty hard to do that without being there. Did Miranda have a job she liked? Was Art paying attention in class? Did Paul look happier now? I had no way of knowing, sitting in my cage at the Brisbanes' house.

Mr. Brisbane tried to entertain me during the day, but it seemed QUIET-QUIET-QUIET compared to Room 26. For one thing, he was out in his workshop a lot, making things out of wood. Or he was at the Senior Center, where he taught other people to make things out of wood. Some evenings he went out and taught wood-craft at the Youth Center while Mrs. Brisbane quietly graded papers.

I had plenty of time to think. Mostly, I thought about Miranda.

And I thought about what a rat I was. I've noticed that humans sometimes called bad people "rats." (I'd like to tell them that the pet rats they sold at Pet-O-Rama were perfectly decent and upstanding rodents.) I knew I was a "rat" because I'd let Miranda take the blame for something I'd done. And I hadn't helped her because I wanted to keep my freedom, so I could come and go as I pleased.

No wonder I'd had trouble eating and sleeping. However, the vitamin chews were just as yummy as Dr. Drew had said.

When Mrs. Brisbane came home, she was full of news about Room 26. She told her husband and me that Mandy, Art and Heidi were all back in school but that Richie and Sayeh were now out sick. Obviously, there was "something" going around . . . and that "something" was not me (thank goodness)!

She also told us that instead of having their homes sitting around on tables, the students had actually put Humphreyville together like a real town. "I think I'd like to move there myself," she told me. "And your statue looks great."

"You must be proud, Humphrey," said Mr. Brisbane. "Not many hamsters have statues built in their honor."

He didn't realize that it was the statue of a rat.

Mrs. Brisbane said that Principal Morales had given permission for me to come back in the classroom. All the parents had been contacted and everyone wanted me back. Of course, she said the kids always did want me back.

"Here's the best news of all. Mandy's mother called and said that she'd read Dr. Drew's report and that she was sorry she blamed you for making her kids sick. She said that they probably just had bad colds. Then, she told me something else."

Mrs. Brisbane paused.

"What?" Mr. Brisbane asked.

"WHAT?" I squeaked.

"She said that in the end, it was a good thing Humphrey went to the vet because her husband ended up getting the job at the veterinary clinic. I guess he'd been out of work for quite a while. She told me to thank him." She turned to me. "Thank you, Humphrey."

I was happy! I was ecstatic (which is a long word that means REALLY-REALLY-REALLY happy). Ordinarily, I would have jumped on my wheel and spun for joy. But for some reason, the more good news Mrs. Brisbane had, the worse I felt. All the nice feelings just made me feel more and more like a rat.

It's not easy being a rat. It's easier to make a decision. And even a rat like me can make the right decision. Of course, I'd always known what the right thing to do was. Deciding to do it was another thing.

Later that evening, after their dinner, the Brisbanes sat near my cage and played a game of dominoes. It seemed like an interesting game with lots of dots on rectangular tiles. They moved the dominoes around, making long rows that crisscrossed the table. Occasionally one of them would shout out, "Good one!" or "Oh, no!"

I took a deep breath. Then, as I had done so many times before, I reached out, jiggled my lock-that-doesn't-lock and opened the door to my cage. I darted out onto the table and danced across the dominoes, figuring I might as well enjoy my last bit of freedom.

Mrs. Brisbane gasped. "Humphrey!"

Just then, I lost my footing on the slick tiles and skidded across a row of dominoes, sending them scattering in different directions.

"Hey! I was winning," said Mr. Brisbane. He scooped me up in his hand and stroked my fur. "Calm down, calm down."

"How on earth did he get out?" Mrs. Brisbane leaned over to inspect the door of my cage. "I guess I didn't close it all the way."

"I guess not." Mr. Brisbane gently put me back in my cage and closed the door. He tested it from the outside. "Now it's closed tightly. Want to try another game?"

"Sure." Mrs. Brisbane turned all the dominoes face-down so I couldn't see any of the dots. She mixed them all up and she and her husband each drew seven tiles—

which they called "bones." Mr. Brisbane drew one tile and put it in the center of the table and the game began.

I stopped to catch my breath. Mrs. Brisbane was convinced that she hadn't closed the door properly. I still had a chance to keep my freedom (and keep being a rat). But I'd made up my mind and there was no turning back.

I waited until there were rows of dominoes going in all directions. Picturing Miranda's face, I pushed my lock-that-doesn't-lock and the door to my cage swung open. I scurried across the table, leaped onto the dominoes, and squeaked, "Don't you get it? Miranda didn't leave my cage door unlocked!"

I knew it sounded like "SQUEAK-SQUEAK-SQUEAK" to the humans, but I had to get my point across.

The Brisbanes looked more than surprised. They looked stunned.

"How did he do that?" Mr. Brisbane asked after a few seconds of silence. "I know that door was locked."

Mrs. Brisbane picked me up. "Humphrey, what are you trying to tell us?"

Mr. Brisbane went over to my cage and fiddled around with the door again. "I don't get it. I just don't get it," he muttered.

He closed the door and joggled it. "It sure seems like it's locked tightly. Hey, I have an idea." He grabbed a pencil from the table and pushed it through the bars of my cage, pushing it against the inside of the lock.

This was one smart man.

He pushed it and nothing happened until he twisted it from the inside, the way I do. Of course, the door swung right open.

"That's it! It looks as if it's locked on the outside, but Humphrey can open it. I wonder how many times he's done that?"

If they only knew!

"I always knew Humphrey was smart," said Mrs. Brisbane.

Mr. Brisbane kept fiddling around with the lock. "It's clearly defective. I guess we'll have to get a new cage."

"Or a new hamster," said his wife. "Just kidding, Humphrey."

She put me back in the cage and Mr. Brisbane closed the door. He wheeled out of the room for a minute and came back with a big piece of wire. "I'll keep it closed for now. The wire will work, but it might be hard for your students to use. And who knows if Humphrey can undo it, too?"

I hoped I could.

Mrs. Brisbane suddenly stood up with a look of horror on her face. "Miranda!" she said with a gasp. "I punished her for not locking the cage and she was sure she did."

"She probably did," Mr. Brisbane agreed.

"Oh, I feel terrible, Bert. She even cried."

So Mrs. Brisbane felt as bad about Miranda as I did.

"Well, nothing's done that can't be undone," Mr. Brisbane said.

He was wrong. There was something done that could never be undone. My freedom and the chance to get out to help my friends were over.

～•～

Mrs. Brisbane decided to keep me home another day so her husband could get me a new cage. I was SAD-SAD-SAD to see my cage all wired up. But I went into my sleeping hut and slept soundly most of the day because I had a clean conscience for the first time in a long time.

I was no longer a rat.

～•～

The new cage looked a lot like the old one, especially after Mr. Brisbane transferred all of my belongings: my seesaw, my tree branch, my climbing ladder, my bridge ladder, my wheel (of course), my water bottle and my mirror—even the cage extension. I held my breath when he took that mirror out of my old cage. After all, I keep the secret notebook and pencil that Ms. Mac gave me behind it.

Luckily, I had planned ahead. The previous night, while the Brisbanes were sleeping, I spent a long time pushing the notebook and pencil against the back of the mirror. They fit perfectly into the little notch behind it. When Mr. Brisbane pulled the mirror out, he didn't even notice the notebook and pencil. He hung the mirror on the side of my new cage. Whew! I might have lost my freedom, but at least I had my notebook and pencil to keep me busy.

Unfortunately, it was Friday, which meant that there was no school the next day, and nowhere to spend the weekend except with the Brisbanes.

It was a nice weekend, mostly quiet except when Bert Brisbane took me out of my cage and set up an amazing maze for me to run. The exercise felt good and I ate some more afterward.

I guess I was healthy after all.

On Monday morning, Mrs. Brisbane covered my cage with a blanket and took me back to school.

Room 26 was strange and yet familiar. For one thing, I'd been away for almost a whole week. For another thing, the houses of Humphreyville had been arranged on tables along the side of the room so it really looked like a town.

Everybody seemed glad to have me back.

"Hiya, Humphrey Dumpty," said A.J.

"I missed you, Humphrey," Sayeh said softly.

"It was lonely here without you," Miranda told me.

"It was hard to sit still without you here," Seth whispered. "But I did a pretty good job."

"BOING-BOING!" Og greeted me. Even the crickets chirped.

The bell rang and my friends settled down in their chairs.

"Boys and girls, before we do anything else today, I have something important to say."

The room was very quiet after those words. "Something important" could mean a pop quiz, a special guest, or someone getting into trouble.

"I'm a teacher, but I'm also a human being. And all human beings make mistakes. I want to tell you about a mistake I made."

There was one small giggle, probably from Gail. Then the room became even quieter.

"A few weeks ago, I accused Miranda of leaving Humphrey's cage open. Because I felt that Humphrey could have been seriously injured, I had to lower her grade. That was my mistake."

I glanced over at Miranda—and so did a number of my friends. She stared at Mrs. Brisbane, her eyes wide with surprise.

"It turns out there was something wrong with the lock on Humphrey's cage. It appeared to be locked, but he was able to open it from the inside. He did the same thing to me that he did to Miranda."

Now all eyes were not on Miranda. They were on me.

"Humphrey has a new cage now with a lock that works. Miranda, I am restoring your good grade."

All eyes turned back on Miranda. She was smiling.

"Most important, class, I want to publicly apologize to Miranda for wrongly accusing her and for not believing what she said was true. She is an honest person and I hope she will accept my apology. Will you, Miranda?"

"Of course, Mrs. Brisbane. I was never sure—"

"*I* am sure," said the teacher. "Now, please take out a piece of paper for our spelling test."

Spelling test! I'd been gone all week and I didn't even know what the words were. I went into my sleeping hut for a nap and slept quite comfortably knowing how happy Miranda was and how happy the whole class was for her.

Miranda—being Golden-Miranda and practically perfect—came over to my cage at the end of the day. "I'm sorry that you're stuck in your cage, Humphrey. I bet you liked your freedom."

Now *that's* why I had to do what I did. "YES-YES-YES," I squeaked out.

"I love you, Humphrey."

Even being locked up in a cage didn't seem so bad after all.

HUMPHREYVILLE REJOICES AS HAMSTER RETURNS TO ROOM 26!

Mrs. Brisbane apologizes to Miranda Golden.

𝕿he 𝕳umphreyville 𝕳erald

In a Tight Spot

That afternoon, feeling rested and raring to go, I crawled out of my sleeping hut because Mrs. Brisbane was going to read to us. She was an excellent reader and was starting a new book that had something to do with pirates and buried treasure. That was interesting to me because I like to bury my treasures (like nuts and other tasty nibbles) in my bedding.

Mrs. Brisbane sat down with the book, but she never did read.

"My glasses!" she said. "Where are my glasses?"

She looked for them on her desk, *in* her desk, in her handbag. Once before, when Mrs. Brisbane lost her glasses, they were actually sitting on top of her head. This time, they weren't there, either.

"Let's do a search," she told the class. My friends ran around the classroom, checking every nook and cranny. It was like a treasure hunt, but they never found the glasses. And believe me, they looked everywhere!

"Sorry, class. I guess I won't be reading today."

My classmates were as disappointed as I was, so Mrs. Brisbane asked Tabitha to read a few pages, followed by Kirk. They are good readers, but not quite as good as Mrs. Brisbane.

Once school was over and the room was empty, Mrs. Brisbane checked the entire room again. "They have to be here, Humphrey," she said. "You haven't seen them, have you, Og?"

Og splashed in his water, and I tried to tell her that I hadn't seen them. Since I couldn't get out of my new cage, I wouldn't be able to help her.

Mrs. Brisbane finally put on her coat and left, muttering under her breath as she did.

When I was sure she was gone, I went to the side of my cage closest to Og.

"Og, I have something to tell you. Are you listening?"

"BOING-BOING!" Og answered.

"Good. I'm glad that Miranda is out of trouble, but now I'm the one in trouble. This new cage they bought me has a lock that I can't open. Mr. Brisbane tested it and made sure of that."

"BOING-BOING-BOING!" Og repeated. He sounded truly alarmed.

"Now I won't be able to come over and have chats with you. And I won't be able to get out and help my friends. Og, my job as a classroom hamster won't be so much fun anymore."

Og dove into the water, splashing furiously. I guess he had heard enough.

"It wasn't right for Miranda to take the blame," I said, talking to myself. "Not right at all."

Og stopped splashing. Everything was silent until I heard the RATTLE-RATTLE-RATTLE of Aldo's cart. He hurried over to my cage. "Welcome back, Humphrey!" he said. "Your pal Og really missed his buddy. Come to think of it, so did I!"

"I missed you, too!" I squeaked loudly.

Aldo pulled up a chair and took out his lunch bag. "We've got some catching up to do. I hear you went to the vet! Richie told me." Repeat-It-Please-Richie is Aldo's nephew. "He said you were healthy as a horse."

Although I wasn't sure I liked being compared to a horse, I knew Aldo meant well.

"Guess what. I went to the doctor, too. And you know how I was tired all the time? Seems like I was low on some vitamins and I was drinking way too much coffee. I'd get a burst of energy and then be even more tired than before! Now I cut back on the coffee, make sure I eat better and I feel like my old self again. Maria and I even went bowling this weekend."

I was glad. Aldo really likes bowling.

"Speaking of vitamins, here's something for you." He took a juicy orange slice out of his bag and pushed it through the bars of my cage.

"I see you got a new cage, too. Looks pretty much like your old cage, but at least you can't get out anymore."

Thanks for reminding me, I thought. Still, Aldo meant well and the orange was extremely tasty.

"You know, a guy like you could get hurt out here in the classroom. You could fall and break something or get caught in a drawer and not have any air. You could be stepped on or sat on or eat something that would make you sick."

Aldo was making me nervous. On the one paw, I'd been out of my cage many times and nothing bad had happened to me. On the other paw, maybe I'd just been lucky!

"Anyway, pal, glad you're safe and sound and back with Og." Aldo folded up his lunch bag and went to work cleaning the room. He worked fast—no napping tonight—which made me GLAD-GLAD-GLAD.

Before he left, Aldo opened the blinds so I'd have light coming from the outside streetlamp. He said good night, turned off the lights and left.

The full moon that night gave the room a soft, silvery glow. I sighed and stared longingly through the bars of my cage. Never again would I slide down the table leg to get to the floor. Never again would I scramble under someone's table to nibble on a nut or to perform one of my extraordinary deeds to help a friend.

As I gazed around the room, I saw something sparkling under Mrs. Brisbane's desk. "Og, look! It's a diamond! Or maybe it's pirate treasure!"

Og splished and splashed.

I stared at the twinkling object. Aldo had probably missed it with his broom. The more I thought about it,

I realized there probably hadn't been any pirates around lately. So what was it?

I kept my eyes on the glittering thing under the desk, and as it started to get light early in the morning, I finally saw what the treasure was: Mrs. Brisbane's glasses!

She had missed them, my classmates had missed them, Aldo had missed them. I hadn't missed them, but now I had no way to recover them and no way to tell anyone where they were.

"Og! Og, wake up!" I said. It's hard to tell when a frog is sleeping because he does it with his eyes open. "I found Mrs. Brisbane's glasses! They're under her desk."

"BOING?"

"If only I had my lock-that-doesn't-lock!"

"BOING-BOING-BOING-BOING!" Og twanged loudly, bouncing up and down. What on earth was my green and lumpy friend trying to tell me?

"BOING-BOING-BOING-BOING!" Og actually hit the top of his glass house.

"Are you trying to get out? What are you saying?" I squeaked.

"BOING-BOING-BOING-BOING-BOING!" Og was going to get a sore throat from all that croaking. Obviously, he wanted me to get Mrs. Brisbane's glasses, but how?

"Okay, okay, I'll try," I squeaked, hoping to stop the racket for a while.

I'd already watched Mr. Brisbane test the cage door, but I decided to try again. I jiggled it, just as I had on my good old lock-that-doesn't-lock. It didn't budge. I pushed up. I pushed down. I pushed with all my might.

The door stayed shut.

"BOING-BOING-BOING-BOING!" Og started up again. I gazed at him through the bars of my cage. He was bouncing higher and higher with each leap and he was twisting and turning in a very unfroglike way. Gail had demonstrated an old dance like that for the class one day. She called it "The Twist."

"BOING-A-BOING-A-BOING-A-SCREEEE!" Again Og twisted himself from side to side. Maybe he needed to see the veterinarian.

Or . . . maybe he wanted me to *twist* the door handle?

I twisted it to the left and I twisted it to the right. I jiggled it and I joggled it. At least Og couldn't say I hadn't tried.

I was getting discouraged—and out of breath—when I had a new idea. I crouched down and got underneath the lock. Then I pushed up with my back and twisted it to the right.

The door flew open so fast, I tumbled out onto the table and did a double somersault.

I'd opened the door! Just as I did, Og leaped so high, he popped the top off his tank . He splashed around in the water with glee. I was a little dazed, but once I got my bearings, I thought about what I had to do. I didn't want to get crushed or trapped or crunched or smashed. As always, I had to have a Plan.

I went over the route in my head for a few seconds.

TICK-TICK-TICK. I checked the clock and realized that school would start soon. It was time for action.

"Wish me luck, Oggy!" I said as I leaned over the side of the table, grabbed onto the top of the table leg and slid to the ground.

The floor was really slick—Aldo must have polished it while I was gone—so instead of running across the floor, I skated as if I were on old Dobbs Pond with Dot. Right paws—slide. Left paws—slide. Right paws—whoa! I spun around in a circle. I slowed down and managed to slide my way to Mrs. Brisbane's desk.

There's just the tiniest space between her desk and the floor. No wonder Aldo had missed seeing the glasses. Only a hamster could fit in such a tiny space. Being a small hamster often comes in quite handy.

I never realized that a pair of glasses could be so large and heavy—at least compared to me. I tried pulling them, but that didn't work. Instead, I moved behind them and PUSHED-PUSHED-PUSHED until they were out on the floor, out in the open. But how was I going to get them back on the desk?

Og was going BOING-BOING-BOING again. I checked the clock. Oops! It was getting dangerously close to school time. Sometimes Mrs. Brisbane comes in early, and I couldn't risk getting caught again. I decided to leave the glasses on the floor, cross my paws that no one would step on them, and get back to my cage. Try as I could, I wasn't getting anywhere *until* I remembered watching kids on sleds after the big snowstorm in January. I threw myself on the floor and slid all the way across on my stomach. You know what? It was fun!

I got back to my table safely. Now came the tricky part. I'd done it before and I could do it again. I had to take a deep breath, grab the long cord hanging down from the blinds and start swinging. I pushed to start the cord swinging. Hanging on tightly, I pushed harder and harder so each swing carried me higher. I tried to ignore that churning in my tummy. There was no time to waste!

At last, I was even with the side of the table. I closed my eyes, took a dive and slid across the table, straight to my cage. Panting, I raced inside and shut the door behind me.

"BOING-BOING-BOING!" said Og.

"Thanks," I squeaked.

At that exact moment, the classroom door opened and the lights came on. Mrs. Brisbane had arrived.

"Good morning," she said. "You fellows are certainly talkative this morning."

She took off her coat and walked toward her desk. All I could think was: PLEASE-PLEASE-PLEASE let her see those glasses!

She walked straight toward them. In fact, it looked as if she was going to walk right over them.

"STOP! LOOK! LISTEN!" I squeaked.

"BOING - BOING - BOING - BOING - BOING!" Og chimed in.

Mrs. Brisbane turned to Og and me. "What on earth are you trying to say?"

Realizing there was nothing to say that she would understand, Og and I became quiet.

Then—oh, joy—Mrs. Brisbane looked down. "My glasses!"

She had a big smile on her face as she picked them up. "Why, I spent last evening tearing up my house looking for these. How did I miss them yesterday?"

She stared down at the glasses. "Aldo might have found them, but he wouldn't have left them on the floor."

Mrs. Brisbane swung around and walked toward Og and me. "I wish you could tell me how they got there."

"Me, too," I squeaked weakly.

Og dove into the water and splashed around.

"Well, all I can say is thank you. And I hope you understand what I'm saying," said Mrs. Brisbane.

She turned and headed back to her desk. "I must be losing my mind. I'm talking to a hamster and a frog," she said softly under her breath.

But I knew she wasn't losing her mind. I was just happy that she'd found her glasses.

MRS. BRISBANE'S EYEGLASSES MYSTERIOUSLY DISAPPEAR!

Just as mysteriously, they reappear the next day.

The Humphreyville Herald

Home Sweet Humphreyville

CLANG-CLANG-CLANG!

"Hear ye, hear ye! The town of Humphreyville welcomes you!" That was A.J., ringing a bell and wearing a funny three-cornered hat. I guess Mrs. Brisbane picked him to be the town crier because he had the loudest voice in the class.

"It's seven o'clock and all is well. Your tour guides will now show you around the town."

After two weeks of excitement and lots of hurried, scurried hard work, Parents' Night finally arrived.

I'm so used to being alone in the quiet classroom with Og on weeknights—with a visit from Aldo—that it was strange but wonderful to see the whole room filled with my classmates' families. I knew most of them from my visits to their houses: A.J. and all the Thomases; the Tugwells; Heidi and Gail and their families; the Rinaldis; the Patels; and all the Golden family (except the dog, Clem, thank goodness), including her mom, dad, stepmom, brother Ben and stepsister Abby.

Even Paul and his mom were there. The class had voted to make him a full citizen of Humphreyville.

Each student got to be a tour guide, showing his or her own family the houses, streets, park and yes, the statue of ME! There was a pleasant hubbub as the families admired the houses. Funny, all the parents thought the very best house was made by *their* own kid!

"Hiya, Humphrey," a familiar voice said. It was Seth's grandmother, Dot Larrabee. She was all dressed up and had bright red lips and fingernails. I hardly recognized her. "Still the daring young man on the flying trapeze?"

I flung myself at my climbing ladder to prove that I was!

After a half hour of *ooh*-ing and *ahh*-ing over Humphreyville, A.J. rang his bell again. CLANG-CLANG-CLANG.

"Hear ye, hear ye!" CLANG-CLANG-CLANG. "The town meeting will now come to order."

A.J. sure liked ringing that bell. He rang it a few more times until Mrs. Brisbane told him that was enough. She asked the parents to take their seats. Mostly, they sat in the kid-sized chairs (though they looked a bit silly). Aldo brought in some folding chairs, too. The students stood so their parents could sit down.

"Mind if I stick around?" Aldo asked.

"I'd be disappointed if you didn't," Mrs. Brisbane told him.

The entire Payne family arrived a little late: Mr. and Mrs. Payne, Mandy, Pammy, Tammy and Bwian. (Brian, of course.) I thought Mrs. Payne worked at night!

CLANG-CLANG-CLANG! A.J. certainly knew how to get people's attention.

"Hear ye, hear ye! Presenting Mrs. Brisbane."

The parents clapped and Mrs. Brisbane came to the front of the room. "It's great to have such a big turnout tonight. I know it's hard to get here after a long day, but I wanted to share with you all the work your children have put into building their own community from scratch. I think they did a wonderful job, don't you?"

The families clapped even louder. A.J clapped, too, and dropped his bell with a large CLANG!

"BOING-BOING!" said Og. Maybe he thought the bell was another frog.

Anyway, everybody laughed. Mrs. Brisbane said it was time to introduce our special guest, Mr. Dudley Dalton, a member of our own town's City Council.

A tall, very thin man with large round glasses and a skinny mustache came to the front of the room. When the clapping stopped, he cleared his throat and pulled a piece of paper out of his suit coat pocket.

"Thank you, uh, Mrs. Brisbane," he said. "I am honored to be here to share this evening with these, uh, wonderful young people of Longfellow School. Truly, they are a, uh, credit to our community."

He smiled slightly, as if smiling hurt his face.

"Since we've had a look at Humpfeeville—I mean Humphreyville—tonight, I'd like to share with you some background about our—uh, own town and how it's grown over the years."

Mr. Dudley Dalton unfolded the paper and began to

read. And read. And READ-READ-READ. Instead of reading something like a story, he read facts and figures, dates and something he called "statistics," which were harder to understand than the hardest vocabulary word we've ever had.

All the parents and students tried hard to concentrate on what Mr. Dalton was saying, but as he went on and on, it was harder to pay attention. If only he made the reading of his statistics as interesting as Mrs. Brisbane makes her stories sound! Soon, I saw Seth start to fidget. His sister, Lucinda, gave him a hard jab in the ribs with her elbow and he settled down again.

Mr. and Mrs. Payne looked a little drowsy, and when I glanced at my friend Dot, I saw that her eyes were closed and her chin was dropping. Didn't Mr. Dudley Dalton notice that he was putting his audience to sleep? I guess not, since he never looked up from his paper, not once.

Everyone tried hard to pay attention until Mr. Dalton got stuck on the word "economics." It's a hard word, I'll admit, but when he said, "eek-o-momics," Gail started giggling. And what's worse, Gail's mom started giggling, too.

Mr. Dalton corrected himself. "Economics. And that pretty much sums up the growth of this wonderful community that we all call home."

He folded up his paper and everyone applauded, probably because they were relieved that he had finished. When everyone clapped, Dot's eyes opened wide, her head jerked up and she said "Oh!" rather loudly. The applause had stopped, so Mrs. Brisbane asked her if she had a question.

Dot stood up. "Not a question, just a comment. Facts and figures are fine, but what makes up a community is people. And I've known some pretty doggone interesting people in my lifetime here."

"Mother," Mrs. Stevenson whispered. *"Sit down."*

"Grandma," Lucinda whispered. *"Please!"*

But Mrs. Brisbane smiled. "I couldn't agree more."

That encouraged Dot to keep going. I was hoping she'd tell the story of the dancing bear.

"For example, when I was growing up here . . ."

Lucinda groaned loudly and Seth squirmed in his chair, but that didn't stop Dot.

"I grew up in a yellow house with white trim down on Alder Street. They were nice houses down there, with big trees around and a store on the corner. Even though it wasn't as big as this room, you could find anything you'd want in that store."

"Where Pet-O-Rama is now!" I squeaked. I hadn't planned on saying anything. It just slipped out. Gail and her mom started giggling again. That didn't stop Dot, either.

"You kids like the mall, but did you know there used to be a roller skating rink there, with an amusement park next door? Had a merry-go-round and a Ferris wheel. Only cost a quarter to get in. Oh, and there were pony rides, too!"

Boy, I have to say, Dot had everyone's attention now. Mr. Dudley Dalton nervously folded and refolded his paper while she talked.

"When you talk about history, you have to know the facts and figures, sure. You also have to know how people lived. What they did, how they thought, what they did for fun." Dot was running out of steam or else she was getting tired of Lucinda tugging on her skirt, trying to get her to sit down. "Anyway, that's my opinion." She sat down. Lucinda, Mrs. Stevenson and Seth all acted pretty nervous, but then a nice thing happened.

People began to applaud. Not for Mr. Dudley Dalton of the City Council, but for Dot. Mrs. Brisbane clapped, too. When the applause died down, Mrs. Brisbane said, "Class, I think we've found our next social studies project. I think we should get out and interview people like Mrs. Larrabee and find out what life used to be like in this town. You can talk to your parents, your grandparents, your neighbors. Mr. Brisbane works down at the Senior Center. I think that would also be a good place to meet people. What do you think, Mr. Dalton?"

"A fine idea," he said, running a handkerchief across his forehead. "People are our, uh, finest resource."

Mrs. Brisbane did a good job of wrapping things up so that people could go home. Instead of leaving, parents and their children gathered around Dot, asking her questions about the amusement park and Alder Street and saying they'd like to get together. Dot's skin was rosy and she was smiling a lot more than when I'd stayed at the house.

"I think Grandma's a star," I heard Seth's mother tell her children.

"Great," said Lucinda, rolling her eyes dramatically.

It turns out that Dot wasn't the only one drawing a crowd. The entire Payne family gathered around my cage. For the first time since I'd known them, they were all smiling at once!

"Here's our guy," said Mrs. Payne.

"Yessir. Humphrey, we owe you our thanks. I'm sorry you had to go to the vet's. But if you hadn't, I never would have gotten that job at the veterinary clinic. A good job, too. Nice people and nice animals," said Mr. Payne.

YIPPEE! He not only got the job, but he liked it!

"I think I'm going to take some classes so I can get promoted," he added.

YIPPEE-YIPPEE-YIPPEE!

"Without you, I wouldn't have been able to go back on the day shift and spend more time with the kids," said Mrs. Payne.

"And I wouldn't have gotten my very own hamster," said Mandy. "You know . . . Winky. He's the cutest hamster I've ever seen. Next to you, of course."

Winky, the toothless, one-eyed hamster, had a real home!

"Thanks, Humphrey. You can come to our house anytime," said Mrs. Payne.

"Next time *I* get to hold him," said Pammy.

"No, *I* get to hold him," said Tammy.

"Me too, me too!" said Brian.

Some things don't ever change, I guess. Winky had his paws full, living at the Paynes' house. Somehow, I knew he could handle it.

⁓

Later that night, after Aldo took away the folding chairs, it was quiet in Room 26 except for the TICK-TICK-TICK of the clock.

I spent some time writing about the evening's events in my notebook. The moon was full and bright. Even in the moonlight, I could see buds of green on the trees outside. The evening was warm. March was almost over, and just as Dot had predicted, it was going out like a lamb.

"Og?" I finally squeaked. "Og, are you awake?"

I heard some gentle splashing, so I knew he couldn't be sleeping.

"Room Twenty-six is a pretty special place, don't you agree?"

Og replied with a friendly, agreeable "BOING."

I glanced across the room. There was the town of Humphreyville spread across several tables. In the moonlight, it looked even more like a real town than during the day. It would all be over soon, of course. Mrs. Brisbane was going to let my friends take their houses home with them. The room would go back to the way it used to be.

I crouched down and pushed up on the lock with all my might. The door swung open.

"It's a lovely night for a stroll," I told Og. "Sorry you can't join me."

"BOING!" Og started bouncing so high, he might as well have been on a trampoline. What was he trying to tell me now?

"BOING-BOING-BOING-BOING-SCREEE!" My old pal did it again. He popped the top off his tank, leaped out and landed on the bag of Nutri-Nibbles nearby.

I must admit, I was worried when I saw him there. It took a lot of effort for him to bounce up high enough to get out of his tank. But how on earth was he going to bounce back in? And if he was out of the water for too long, he could be in big trouble. But he was already out of his tank and there wasn't a thing I could do about it except enjoy his company.

"It's a lovely night for a stroll," I repeated. "And I'm so glad you can join me!"

Og and I scurried along our table until we reached Humphreyville. The table it was on was quite a bit lower than ours. I remembered what Aldo had said about broken bones, so instead of jumping, I lowered myself by my paws and dangled there for a second, then gently dropped down. I landed pretty hard and even did a somersault, but we hamsters are good acrobats. Og had no problem making the big leap.

There we were, on the main street of Humphreyville:

Taco Boulevard. For the first time, I realized that the houses were just the right size for a hamster like me or for a frog like Og. We strolled past A.J.'s house of blocks, which was next door to Miranda's purple castle. Across the street was a long drawing of shops, a movie theater, a bowling alley—even a pet store—which all my friends had worked on.

We turned down Basketball Avenue, past Garth's log cabin, which was next door to a small house with a large basketball court. That was Tabitha's house, naturally. She loved sports more than anything. On Soccer Street, we saw Seth's rocket ship house. Sayeh's apartment building stood across from Art's amazing merry-go-round house with the slide coming down and the train tracks going through it. Across the street was a smaller version of Art's house. It was Paul's place, of course.

Video Game Way crossed at the corner and there was Gail's bright yellow house with a picket fence around it and flowers painted on it. Pizza Place had a pizza parlor as well as the courthouse, with its cardboard pillars and a clock up on top. On this clock, it was always twelve o'clock. That meant it was either noon or midnight. Next to the courthouse was the school and playground.

We turned down Recess Lane, which led to the large park and the playground and a baseball diamond. The grassy Og the Frog Nature Preserve had been moved to one side of the park.

"Nice sign," I said. Og twanged in agreement.

We stopped in the center of the park and stared up at the tall statue. There I was, larger than life—and golden! Even a Golden Hamster was never that golden before. On the base of the statue it read: "To Humphrey. A friend in need is a friend indeed."

It's a funny kind of saying, but I thought about it and realized it's true. March had roared in like a lion, blowing in a whole lot of trouble for the students in Room 26. Seth's jitters, Art's failing grades, Mandy's unhappy family, and especially Miranda's punishment for something she didn't do. These were my friends and I did my best to help them. Now March was ending and all those troubles had blown away with the blustery winds.

Tomorrow, Humphreyville would be gone. But my friends would still be there and Mrs. Brisbane, Aldo and Og as well.

We walked through town and headed back for our table. I was relieved to see that Og had no trouble hopping up on the table. He then leaped to the Nutri-Nibbles bag, bounced his way up to the top and then, with one enormous leap, jumped back into the tank, where he landed with a very impressive splash!

"Well done, Oggy!" I complimented him. Of course tomorrow, Mrs. Brisbane would find the top off his tank and wonder about it, but somehow I wasn't worried.

Once I was back in the safety of my cage, I felt unsqueakably happy.

"You know what, Og? We turned out to have the BEST-BEST-BEST jobs of all! The classroom pets of Room Twenty-six!"

"BOING-BOING-BOING-BOING!" Og agreed.

I'm absolutely positive that he was saying, "Yes!"

FAMILIES PROCLAIM HUMPHREYVILLE
TO BE THE PERFECT COMMUNITY!

Students say they'll always think of
Humphreyville as their hometown.

𝕿he 𝕳umphreyville 𝕳erald

Humphrey's Tips for Staying Out (and Getting Out) of Trouble!

1. If you make a mistake and get in trouble, it's always a good idea to admit you're wrong and say you're sorry.
2. Sometimes you get in trouble for something you didn't do. Try and stay calm, but squeak up for yourself and explain what really happened. (This doesn't always work, but you can TRY-TRY-TRY.)
3. If you get in trouble and lie about it, you'll only get in more trouble, so always squeak the truth!
4. When a good friend (like Miranda) gets in trouble, sometimes you feel as bad as your friend does. That's what friends are for.
5. When a good friend (like Art or Seth) gets in trouble, a good friend (like Paul or me) can sometimes lend an ear—or a paw—and help out.
6. When a friend (like Og) warns you that you're about to get in trouble—listen!
7. If people do something mean, like get you in trouble or even get you banished from your classroom, remember: They may have an even *bigger* problem than you do.
8. If you think you have troubles, think of someone worse off than you are, like my friend Winky, the reject hamster (whose troubles are happily now over).